The sound set the [...]
end. He forced himsel[...]

They stood in rows like gaming pieces up-ended in the sand, in armor that might as well be empty for all the animation they showed. The face plates were screened, reflecting a charcoal emptiness back at him. Jack was afraid, deathly afraid, because he knew what was going to happen next.

The armor groaned. It was a sound that came from deep in the earth, vibrating upward through stone layers and sand, and Jack shuddered to hear it. He needed to get into his own armor, for protection and power, but he stood, rooted.

The armor facing him represented men he'd trained with and led, but these were no longer men. And then he heard it, the noise of a suit of armor tearing apart, as the beast within burst out.

Huge. Bigger than the armor, cloaked in shreds of bone and flesh that had once been human, the great gray-green reptile smashed forth. White teeth flashed and red eyes burned, and a frill went up as the berserker charged Jack. . . .

DAW Titles by Charles Ingrid:

BOOK TWO OF THE SAND WARS

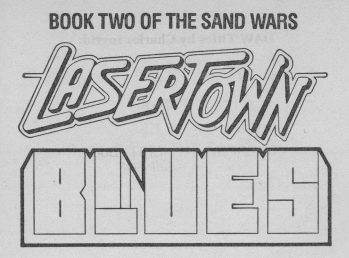

LASERTOWN BLUES

CHARLES INGRID

DAW BOOKS, INC.

DONALD A. WOLLHEIM, PUBLISHER

1633 Broadway, New York, NY 10019

DAW Book Collectors No. 735.

First Printing, February 1988

1 2 3 4 5 6 7 8 9

PRINTED IN THE U.S.A.

To my editor, Sheila Gilbert, with many thanks, and to the wonderful Wollheim organization.

PART 1

PART I

CHAPTER 1

"No suit, no soldier. It's as simple as that." The bullet-nosed D.I. looked down the row of men who sat before him, their shoulders bare and sweaty against a too white sun. "We can hand you a laser rifle, but you'll never be a soldier."

It was not really as simple as that. It never was. Still, the men sat there, covered in alien dust, and listened to the D.I. One, a man not-old and not-young, shivered involuntarily, feeling naked under the Malthen sun, for he hadn't been out of his armor much in the last six weeks. His skin, also too white, began pinking rapidly. They'd been shucked out of their armor after days on patrol, drilled and exercised while their equipment had been racked and taken away.

Young men, not much older than boys, flanked him on either side, their gazes intent upon the drill instructor. But Jack Storm had been in this situation before and though his jaw tensed along with the others, he didn't quite feel what they felt. He'd mustered up good enough to wear battle armor years ago—now he only wondered if he was good enough to join the Emperor's personal guard. And unlike the others sitting in the rows in front of and behind him, he wasn't here out of any patriotic sense that he owed his service to the Emperor. On the contrary. He felt keenly that the Emperor owed him.

He was twenty years older than most of them. His body didn't show it though, for he'd spent seventeen of those years adrift in cryogenic suspension. As he sat cross-legged in the courtyard and listened to the D.I.'s voice bounce off the incredible, forty-foot-high walls that surrounded them there on the parade grounds, the sweat dripped off his lean body and puddled to the ground. His sandy colored hair slicked back darkly. His high cheek-boned face was tanned, to the neckline, for the recruits only wore their helmets half-time, and the Malthen sun was quick to darken their skins any time they were exposed to it.

Jack squinched his pale blue eyes closed for a second, shutting out everything. As quickly, he opened them, not liking what he'd felt for that fraction of a second. *The dead blue-black sleep of cryogenics, cradling him, killing him, for seventeen years. . . .* He reminded himself that there were days when that curse was almost a blessing. A forty-odd-year-old body wouldn't have made it through the last six grueling weeks.

The man next to him shifted. He tossed a smokestick butt into the dust. "What's he leading up to?"

10

"You'll see," Jack answered quietly. He resisted the impulse to look back, and up two stories, to the offices overlooking the parade ground, where the whippet-lean man would be watching today, as he had every day, the volunteers in training. The man, a legendary mercenary handpicked by the Emperor to form this guard, had no name, just as Jack Storm had no age. The Owner of the Purple knew Jack well—but even that friendship held no sway with the D.I.

The D.I.'s arrogant gaze swept over them. "All right, men. We all know only one out of every four of you will make it to the Emperor's Guard. What you don't know is when or how that decision will be made." He crossed his arms over his gleaming silver chest. "Today's the day. You've been graded by your performance for the last few weeks. Today is wash out day. Your suits were given to you and you were shown how to maintain them. The final determination will be made *based on the condition of your suits*. They're being stripped down and evaluated right now."

"Fuck," muttered the redhead to Jack's right.

The sentiment echoed inside Jack, too. They'd just come in off three days' patrol with no chance to charge or repair their gear. Just what the hell did these people expect?

But under Jack's first conscious dismay, a deeper thought channeled. The corner of his mouth quirked up in a wry smile. The man who respected his gear, who planned for and maintained a reserve, who could repair his suit better than an unfamiliar mechanic—that was the sort of man Emperor Pepys wanted at his back.

And that philosophy just might have been the death knell to all of Jack's ambitions. His suit was an antique compared to the equipment most of these youngsters used. His suit was the forerunner, the prototype that this new equipment was based on. His suit had gone to the Sand Wars and come back.

And his suit was alive.

Jack gave an involuntary shiver as the D.I. boomed, "Dismissed!" How deep into his suit could they delve? He licked his lips. They were dusty. He tasted an alkaline tang. The farm boy left behind in his past told him this soil couldn't be fertile. It was a good thing they were soldiering on it instead. A shadow fell over his thoughts.

A broad, callused hand reached down for Jack. He took it and got to his feet.

"Cold beer?"

Jack shrugged, as someone in the milling group bumped him slightly. "Why not. It's going to be a wait. They've got over three hundred suits to test."

He fell in beside the chunky, dark-skinned man who'd stood over him. He didn't know Daku well, although he was in his late twenties, one of the oldest volunteers there, outside of Jack.

Rank hadn't been allowed in basic training. Daku might be a five star general or a civilian. He'd worked, trained, shoulder to shoulder with Jack for weeks without a word. Now Daku looked across his shoulder at Jack. An unreadable expression flickered over his dark face. His broad nose wrinkled slightly at the bridge. "Worried?"

"Yeah. You?"

Daku nodded. "Although," he observed, "there are some who should not wonder at their fate. Those that used their equipment roughly, figuring it will go to scrap, while they are chosen and go on to new suits and new ranks ... well, for those, it will be a foregone conclusion."

They were buffeted by the ranks of the trainees as they reached the double doors to the outside. Daku took the crowding good-naturedly, even as Jack shrank back a little. He disliked crowds.

Jack changed quickly in the locker room. He wore a pair of serviceable gray pants with many pockets, and a loose, flowing shirt. Daku wore dark colors, as dark as he was, and as Jack joined him, he reflected briefly that he wouldn't want to meet Daku in one of Malthen's back alleys. Hover taxis were waiting outside the lockers ... in response to the scores of calls from the training grounds, a fleet of them had come to meet the obvious need.

He and Daku picked an automatic unit and got in. Daku paused, his finger poised to punch coords into the computer board. "Where?"

Jack shrugged. "Wherever."

Daku punched out a series and they sat back, speeding downhill from the Emperor's rose-pink complex, toward the belly of the beast known as Malthen, the city for which the planet had been named.

* * *

Daku waited until after the second round of beer had been served, then he leaned forward in the quiet bar. The booth creaked a little under his solid weight.

"And what about you? You don't seem worried."

Jack flicked a nail against his cold glass. The neat scar along his right hand, where the little finger had been sheared off, ached. It served as a reminder that the frost of cold sleep could injure, even kill. He wondered what the other volunteer wanted from him—why Daku had singled him out. Even as Daku had been assessing him, Jack had been weighing the dark man. This was not a cheap bar. None of the other trainees had come here. Nor was it a street bar, filled with mercenaries and other outlaws, or street toughs. Jack looked up, wondering just how friendly he wanted to become with this potentially dangerous man. For a moment, he wished he had the Purple with him, but the commander had agreed their friendship would be off-limits during Basic. The Owner of the Purple had recommended Jack to Emperor Pepys himself, and gotten him the appointment to the training program. From there, Jack's fate was in his own hands—just exactly where he liked it.

A man walked in the front door of the bar and stood a moment, half-shadowed. He drew first Jack's glance, and then Daku's.

Daku's mouth quirked. "Just a Walker."

Jack stirred in the booth. The man was armed, discreetly, but heavily, and that nagged at him.

Walkers were a radical sect that had sprung from the old Terran religion called Christianity, and they were dedicated to finding anthropological and archaeological proof that Jesus Christ went on to walk other worlds. Still, Jack had never seen an armed one before. The sight tugged at his mind. A militant Walker would be everybody's concern. The man spoke softly to the bartender and then faded into one of the back rooms.

Daku grunted. Then he emptied his glass. "Well, Jack, you're taking it coolly. I might almost think you'd been through this before."

To keep his companion placated, he murmured, "There's a lot at stake, but sweating won't make it happen." He had no intention of telling the dark man that he *had* been through all this before. He wasn't listed in any of the Dominion computer records. Nothing existed to designate him as the last fighting survivor of the Sand Wars on Milos except his battle-scarred memories, and he intended to keep it that way. It had been twenty years ago, ancient history to most, but not to him. Not to a man lost in cryogenic sleep and hooked up to a military debriefing loop, where he relived every step of the Sand Wars in dreams to which there had been no end—no end to the point where he'd lost nearly every other memory of another life, of his existence before he'd become an infantry Knight. He existed now for one reason and one reason only. Revenge. All he had to do was keep finding the pieces and putting them together. He hoped this man was one of them.

"That is true," Daku replied. He lifted his glass and took a long draft of beer.

Out of the corner of his eye, Jack saw a young woman come into the bar. She was lithe and graceful, and had the quickness of a street acrobat. Her tawny hair, wild about her pretty face, and her sleek, dark blue jumpsuit bespoke her reason for being in a bar this early. She had all the earmarks of a high-class prostitute. Jack frowned as her gaze flicked his way and then passed him by, as she went to the bar rather than a table and sat.

Daku set the glass down. "So where have you come from, with such high hopes," he prodded.

Jack looked back to him. So this was going to be a show me yours and I'll show you mine session, he thought briefly. He hesitated only slightly before pulling out a photo and slapping it down on the table, and answering, "I rangered there." He watched for the other's reaction.

Daku sucked in his breath as his fingers pulled the photo closer. "Where did you get this?"

"I bribed a member of the survey team."

"It's not a pretty sight."

Jack didn't respond. It wasn't. The sight of a once verdant, beautiful planet reduced to a char was beyond description. To Jack, the only hope in the photo was that the dark blue seas and vaporous clouds still remained.

"This place was firestormed."

"Yes."

Daku pushed the photo back. "The only one I've heard of recently was Claron. No warning."

"No reason." Except perhaps to wipe out Jack. A nerve ticked along his jaw line. First Milos, to the Thraks, and then Claron, to firestorm. Vengeance needed, twice over.

"There's always a reason. We just don't know it yet." The dark face paled a little. Then Daku said, "That was a bad affair."

"Yeah." Bad was an understatement. Memories flooded Jack, memories of waking up to a firestorm inferno and escaping while an entire planet burned. He pushed them back. "Where are you from?"

"Africa Two," the man said and it was Jack's turn to feel surprised. The all black planet rarely dealt with the Triad systems. Segregated by choice and desire, African Twos were seldom friendly toward other systems. It seemed vastly out of character for a citizen to be interested in serving Emperor Pepys as a guard. Daku sensed his reaction and said, "I don't like Thrakian warships in our space."

That was a philosophy Jack could second. Despite treaties, enemies should stay enemies. He did, holding up his glass. "Death to all Thraks," he said softly, proposing treason in his toast. He cared little if he revealed himself. It was the threat of Thrakian swarms that had made him leave his farm on Dorman's Stand and volunteer for the army in the first place. He had little enough memory left of his family and home planet.

"Amen," answered Daku and they drained their glasses.

"Ever see a Thrakian sand planet?" Daku asked casually.

Jack had. He'd been there on Milos, fighting, while the Thraks terraformed the planet into a vastness of dunes, sands to be filled with their eggs for hatching. But he couldn't answer without giving himself away. He took a long draught of beer before answering, "No."

"I have. Dorman's Stand, one of the last to go under. It'd eat away at you, tell you that. A dead planet now, for all that it's a nursery to Thraks."

His home. His family. His fields and orchards, ground to dust and sand. His hand clenched around his beer glass, and to distract himself, Jack watched the amber-haired blonde at the bar shrug off a potential customer. Her gaze flickered briefly over Jack. He cleared his throat, hoping that Daku hadn't noticed. He checked his watch as his drinking companion began to slip his card into the table slot to order another round of drinks. He held up his palm. "That's enough for me. I want to get back."

Daku looked up. He smiled pleasantly. "But there's no need to worry, Jack. You won't be going back. I've been sent to turn you back into the clay we are all made of. Dust to dust."

He looked into a needle-nosed palm laser. Jack reacted before he knew he was going to react. He dropped down, kicked the table up into Daku's teeth, and rolled out of the way of the spray of fire. The blonde at the bar screamed and tables rang as they overturned, the area clearing as customers hit the deck.

As Jack dove into a shadowy corner and skidded into a crouch, Daku got to his feet. Blood poured from his upper lip. The palm laser shook.

"You won't get out of here. It's not my job to let you go."

Jack ducked as laser fire crisped the booth behind his head. He kissed the floor as sprinklers went on and a fine mist drifted down in response to the assault. He could hear Daku move to another position.

The blonde crawled over to Jack and slipped him a handgun. "What would you do without me?"

"Live alone," he said. "Now find a corner and stay the hell out of the way."

She gave him a pout and crawled past him as ordered.

"I suppose you won't tell me who hired you." Jack paused and calculated possible moves.

Daku just grinned. The blood from his lip stained his jowls a dark purple, giving him a feral look. He pivoted around, spraying deadly fire as he moved. But Jack had already jumped six feet to the left. A shielding table melted into a puddle of plastic which smoked and a choking smell filled the air.

Daku crouched, believing he was out of Jack's sight, and mopped his lip with the back of his hand. He checked the charge in his gun. Jack watched him uneasily, knowing that he could end it all right there except that he was against shooting a man in the back, and he wanted to know why he was a target.

Jack dove for his enemy. He barreled into the assassin, sliding him out onto the floor. "Who hired you? Who did it?" He knew it was a mistake the moment he wrapped arms about the other. Daku bunched his shoulders and Jack felt the massive strength of the other as the killer's muscles flexed. He wasn't going to be able to hold on long enough to save his life.

Daku twisted a forearm up, palm laser glinting in the half-light of the bar. He fired, twice, the laser fire scorching Jack with its heat—and piercing Daku's own skull.

"Dammit," Jack whispered hoarsely. "Who hired you!" The light faded from scornful eyes before Daku could answer. Jack let go.

The blonde was at his side before the body finished bouncing. "Let's get out of here," she nudged him. "This neighborhood has too much class to take this kind of action quietly. The Sweepers will be all over us."

Outside, in the hover taxi, he finally took a breath. "What made you follow me?"

"Are you kidding? Wash out day and you're not with me trying to find out what's happening to Bogie?" She wrinkled her nose, suddenly looking like the street urchin she'd recently been, and much younger than her made-up face would indicate. "C'mon. I'm not psychic for nothing. Besides, Daku's gone out of his way to ignore you for the last six weeks . . . now he gets chummy? So I knew that you had gone fishing and decided to see what you'd reeled in. What do you think? Assassin or just someone trying to eliminate competition for the Guard?"

Jack took a disposable tissue from the hover taxi dashboard and held it out to her. "I think you're wearing too much makeup. You look like a tart."

CHAPTER 2

The Owner of the Purple sat, looking just as
Jack had imagined him, whippet-lean and handsome, his silver hair combed back from his forehead. He drummed the arm of his swivel chair
impatiently. From the darkened booth overlooking the parade grounds, Jack could see the men
milling restlessly down below and a steady,
antlike line of newcomers joining the waiters.
He knew that test results would start dribbling
in soon. The tension in the air was growing
thick enough to cut. He watched the grounds,
distracted, until Purple asked, "Is it paranoia,
Jack, or do you think that Daku was out for you
specifically?"

Jack's attention snapped back to the commander. "He said it was his job. I think that's
specific enough."

"We won't be able to trace him back."

"No," Jack answered briefly.

Amber shot him a glowing smile, and point-
edly got up and sat down next to the window
overlooking the parade grounds. She'd let him
know when the action started.

He looked back to his friend, once a free mercenary opponent, then a companion, and now a superior officer. "That's where they made their mistake ... African Twos are deadly assassins, but they also let their egos get in the way. I might have thought Daku was just trying to eliminate competition for the Guard until he told me otherwise."

"Then ... why today? Why not a training accident during Basic? We've lost several volunteers."

Jack shrugged. "Maybe he was hoping to get a suit out of it. You're going to be screening against potential smugglers among the wash outs today anyhow. Maybe Daku wasn't against turning a buck any way he could. Battle armor would be worth a lot to a freebooter."

The Purple smiled. "And besides ... you're good in a suit. He might not have had the opportunity before today."

"There's that." Jack relaxed into his chair. The Purple knew how it was with battle armor—he owned his own, a mauve-colored suit that was even more of a relic than Jack's. Like his own soldier of fortune origins, the purple suit's history was lost in the mists of war. He thought about the man who'd tried to kill him. "If Daku had been another mercenary, his employers might have been worried about connections with you or me."

"There's that, too," the Purple said. The smile thinned. "Mercenaries don't hit other mercenaries. We face off often enough doing work, as it is."

In the underworld where the two of them had met, employment for private wars and aggravations was the work they did—and it was a foregone conclusion that the mercenary who protected your back today might well be facing you over a rifle tomorrow.

Purple said quietly, "The word at the bar is that it was a righteous shoot. You won't even be questioned. Tapes show what happened. Pepys has already reviewed them and dismissed any charges."

He'd forgotten how dry his mouth could get. "That's good." He needed the Guard. Even the Purple had no idea of who he really was, where he'd really come from—or what he really wanted. Only Amber had been let that far into his soul.

"Jack," Amber said softly. "Almost everyone is assembled down there."

The Purple tapped his fingers again and checked his watch. "It's about time." He looked at the young woman. "It's a good thing Jack kept you hidden from the other recruits, or Daku might have gone through you first."

"If he'd tried," Amber retorted, "he'd have been dead that much sooner."

The Purple's silver-black eyebrows arched. "Jack, as her guardian, I think you should watch yourself. Daku could have been hired by her former pimp."

Amber started. "Rolf wasn't a pimp!"

"Svengali, then. We both know that Rolf's connections are many. He didn't like giving you up, Amber, and despite the order from the Emperor, isn't likely to let you go."

"He didn't have any choice."

"No, but I've been led to believe he had quite a stake in Amber, though neither of you have seen fit to let me know what it was."

Amber would not look at Jack, and Jack wasn't going to betray her here. She was deeply ashamed that her former guardian had subverted her psychic talents into the ability to kill. She'd been trained subliminally to be an assassin—but neither she nor Jack knew who Rolf's targets had been, and she had no intention of ever being used in such a way.

Jack stirred. He was more concerned about enemies buried deeply in the Emperor's organization. He already had one name and a face: Commander Winton, the man who had ordered entire battalions to be abandoned on the surface of Milos. "Daku could have been hired by someone trying to track us down. It's part of the charm of being a bodyguard—no wrist chips for the master system. We operate outside the computer records and there's bound to be more than one of us with a colorful past."

"Yes that's a distinct possibility. There are no records of you—or your suit." The Purple smiled again, that thin elegant smile. "I have a similar problem." He swung his chair about abruptly, looking down at the grounds as Amber made a sound. "You're going to be late. I suggest you hurry."

"I'll do that." Jack got to his feet. He saluted sharply. "With your permission, sir."

"Go on. I'll keep Amber up here with me, if you don't mind."

Storm grinned. "I have little to say about it. Just make sure *she* doesn't mind." He closed the observation office door on Purple's dry chuckle, feeling uneasy. He and the officer had discussed Amber's role in his life and he didn't like leaving her alone with Purple. He shrugged. Amber could handle herself.

Amber swung around to look at the silver-haired man who ran the Emperor's personal guard. Jack felt a loyalty to this man, won fairly in combat situations they'd seen as mercenaries against, and then with, one another. She didn't feel the same loyalty. She kept her street wariness honed like a fine blade. It helped her to survive.

She crossed her legs. "I know this isn't social."

"No. And it has nothing to do with today's events, exactly. What happened to Jack today didn't help any, but it clarified the situation a little."

Amber felt a sudden chill across her bare arms. She chafed them in response. "What is it? I don't like what you've done to him. He has a whole new mindset."

"It's you. Your relationship with Jack is a liability he can't afford if he makes the Guard, and we'll both be damn surprised if he doesn't. These last weeks have been spent fine-tuning Jack back into what he used to be—an unstoppable weapon that only needs to be pointed in the right direction. He hasn't time to foster you."

Amber gave a wry smile, one that never quite reached the coldness of her golden brown eyes.

"You mean I'm a chink in his battle armor, so to speak."

The Purple smiled back. "Well put. Yes. He's going to have to ask you to let him move on. There're separate quarters for the Guard ... you'll be left in his old quarters, no problem there. And you'll be provided for."

She stopped rubbing her arms and simply held herself, bracing herself for the impact of the commander's words. She looked at him. "Suppose I don't want to be left alone."

The Purple looked away. He stood up and moved to the window, watching the recruits down below. "Jack may make a mistake he can't afford by keeping you."

The iciness seemed to have reached her chest. Amber swallowed tightly. "I'll stay behind if he asks me—but he won't. Jack needs me in ways you couldn't even begin to imagine." She clenched her teeth, on the brink of telling this arrogant bastard some of the basis for their being together ... such as her being the only one who could control his maneater of a suit. But she stopped herself.

The commander did not turn back around. He merely said, "But you will let me go."

"If he asks. Which he won't." Amber jabbed at a small pool of wetness that insisted on leaking from one eye. "Now let's just shut up and see if he makes the Guard, all right?"

The silver-haired man crossed his arms and said nothing further.

* * *

Jack wished he could dismiss the prickle of unease that ran up his spine as he took the elevator down to the parade grounds. Chillingly, he'd noted that the Purple hadn't asked who could have been behind the attack or why if it wasn't because of Amber. It was the sort of question you didn't ask another mercenary. It was axiomatic in the business that you made a few enemies.

The elevator shussed open in front of him. Jack rubbed the scar of his missing finger thoughtfully. The tale of his service as a veteran in the Sand Wars—a war which had been lost when it should have been won—and the knowledge of the cover-ups surrounding it, and his own survival, when all others had died, made him a liability. Which was why Jack kept his mouth shut. It seemed healthier that way.

The sun blasted him as soon as he set foot on the parade ground sands. A gritty brown sand, unique to Malthen, it clung to his boots and wafted every time he took a step. If he had a credit for every grain of it he'd ever brushed out of his suit's circuits—

A murmur rose on the crowded grounds. "Here come the equipment racks!"

Jack felt his own heart drum. The suits were being brought back in. What would he find? Had his own armor survived the testing? Had the uniqueness of his equipment been discovered—or destroyed—by the procedure? Jack's lips went dry.

He had to make the Guard. It was his only way to survive in the Triad system without going back to being a free mercenary. And it was where he had to be to ask the questions he needed to ask. It was the place he had to be to hunt down Winton and find out the truth about the Sand Wars. It was the best way he could curry favor and win aid for his plans to revitalize Claron. His hand balled into a fist. He would find the answers he wanted. Or die trying. And he didn't forget that he nearly had, less than an hour ago.

He pushed his way to the rack with the other volunteers.

The white armor hung there, catching the rays of the sun, and projecting the reflection with an aura of its own. It was a little sleeker than the newer models, the Flexalinks were of a different alloy, and the helmet hanging on the meathook above it had more face plate. It also carried repaired crimps and, on the chest, a duller paint hid the insignia he'd painted there . . . oh, some twenty years ago. When he wasn't much younger physically than he was now.

Jack grabbed a gauntlet and pulled the suit closer.

Hi, boss.

The sentience within the suit greeted him, and Jack let out his breath in a ragged sigh. Whatever tests the armor had undergone, the microscopic being determinedly regenerating itself inside Jack's suit still lived.

He wasn't sure how he greeted that knowledge. The nightmare of Milos haunted him every time he wore the suit . . . but it had become a drug he couldn't do without when making war. The Milots had salted the suits of the Knights with a parasite. It infested the men who wore the suits on a long-term basis, and eventually cannibalized them, and then finally burst out of the shell of the armor itself—a full blown, lizard berserker warrior unafraid of death. The Milots had thought the berserkers could save them when the Knights could not. They'd been wrong on all counts.

And they'd created part of the nightmare which had led the Dominion to abandon their troops on Milos. The infected men and suits had been scourged, by leaving them to the Thraks. Only a minor effort to pick up the troops had been made, to save face, and with the knowledge that the pullout was doomed to be stopped by the Thrakian warships ringing the planet. Whoever had calculated that eventuality had been dead right—except for one troopship which had made it through, even though it was vitally damaged.

Jack knew only that the parasite wasn't in him. Amber sensed it, could single out the growing soul. It was in the suit. But when he wore the suit, it enhanced his already considerable abilities. It invaded him. It made him invincible.

And he needed that to extract the revenge he sought.

"Hi, Bogie," he whispered back mentally. "Rough time?"

Th' worst. Where's Amber? I lost her.

"She was helping me out." Jack paused as Garner, the recruit next to him, grinned.

"Glad to get the old suit back, huh, Storm."

Garner pulled his rack close. "You have to work miracles with that junk to keep up with us."

Jack shrugged off the volunteer's sneer.

"Cut it out, Garner," a voice said at Jack's back. "And, obsolete or not, that suit can power walk circles around you."

"Maybe. Ask him what happened to the guy who went out for a beer with him this morning, eh?"

Jack backed out of the skirmish, dragging the rack behind him, thinking of the suit that had trailed him across the galaxy. It was old enough to have been left him by his father. As far as his fellow recruits—and even the Purple—were concerned, it had been.

Garner wouldn't leave well enough alone. He followed after, still leering. "You know what they say about you? They call you Silent Jack. You're no team player. Yeah, that's it. You always know more than you say. A helluva lot more."

Jack met the narrowed gaze of the other. "We're down to count zero on this one, Garner. If you'd wanted to eliminate me from the finals, you had your chance. Now I suggest you stay clear of me."

A breeze must have shaken the suit on its rack because the right gauntlet lifted and wavered on its own. Garner's face whitened and he pivoted away. Jack grabbed for the gauntlet.

Lemme at him, boss.

"Forget it, Bogie." But Jack's stomach muscles went tight. He was losing control of the suit—and Bogie was gaining the ability to animate himself. The psychic safeguards Amber had put up were giving way—and Jack knew that his life was on the line now, every time he climbed into the battle armor.

One of his last coherent memories of the Sand Wars was seeing a suit split open . . . a creature burst forth from the cadaverous remains of someone who'd been a friend and a soldier under Jack's command. . . .

"Gentlemen . . . FALL IN!"

The ranks of recruits swelled across the parade ground, doubled by the equipment racks at their sides. Battle armor gleamed and reflected the sun's glory, dwarfing the men next to their suits. The D.I. rode a portable cherry picker, just to oversee them. His stony jaw locked as the men came to attention in formation.

There was no need to ask for silence. Here and there was a metallic clang as battle armor swayed in the wind and hit the equipment rack holding it.

Jack put one hand out to his rack, more to steady himself than his suit. Even that close a touch brought Bogie's mental voice into his thoughts.

What's up, Boss?

"Not now."

A sulky withdrawal replaced the eagerness. Jack resisted the temptation to look back, and up, to the booth overlooking the grounds, to Amber. What had happened to her control over Bogie's sentience? Unless Bogie was just growing too strong for her to influence. . . .

"Gentlemen. As I call your name, fall out. Leave

your suits behind on the rack. You will be issued a paycheck in the locker room."

The hair on the back of Jack's neck crawled, in spite of himself. In a silence as cold as the cryogenic sleep that had dominated nearly half his life, he waited for his name to be called and never heard it.

The men left behind in a field of battle armor stirred unbelievingly as the D.I.'s voice faltered. Then the tyrant of their basic training cleared his throat.

"The rest of you raise your right hands and repeat after me: I hereby swear loyalty in all manner of life and thought to the Emperor Pepys as a member of the Dominion Knights and his personal bodyguard . . ."

Jack raised his right hand and lied with every word he spoke echoing across the parade grounds.

CHAPTER 3

Amber's face was pale. "What do you mean, I'm not going with you?"

"I'll be in the barracks. I don't even know what rank I'm going to be assigned yet. The barracks is no place for you. The Purple agrees with me—it's better for you to stay here. You're still on palace grounds and you'll have all the same privileges you did before—"

"I'll be alone."

"No, you won't. Whenever I'm off duty, I'll be here, or you'll be there. And this way, you'll have the time to go back to school and the privacy to study."

She bit her lower lip. "I don't want to go back to school."

"You've got to. If you're ever going to be anything more than the thief Rolf tried to turn you into—"

"Assassin. Not thief. Don't forget it."

Jack met her eyes and saw the hurt welling up in them. "I haven't forgotten it. But he doesn't control you any more."

"No." She balled her slender hands up. "Jack, I want to go with you and Bogie. I don't want to be alone—"

"You're too young."

"Too young for what? I've seen more on Malthen's streets than you ever—why, shee-it! You're just a farm boy!"

Jack felt the corner of his mouth pull, in spite of himself. She was right, of course, unfailingly. He was just a farm boy from Dorman's Stand who'd become a Dominion Knight and then a ranger and then a mercenary—and he wouldn't have survived Malthen without her savvy. He brushed a tawny strand of hair from her face. That face. Capable of looking as young as a twelve year old and as old as his mother. But it wasn't the face that bothered him. And he didn't know how to tell her.

"Look at it this way. You've graduated from my protection service."

"But what if I don't want to?" She rubbed a knuckle quickly across her eyes. "And what about Bogie! Who's going to keep him in line? What's to keep him from eating you up and spitting out your bones?"

Jack felt uneasy now. He shook his head, saying, "I don't know. But he's strong enough now to break out from your repression. If he's that strong—I'll either have to take my chances or. . . ."

"Or what?"

Jack shrugged. He picked up his duffel.

Amber stomped her foot. "Don't you walk out of here!"

He turned back. His head tilted to one side as he considered her. "Or what?"

"Or—or—dammit, how should I know! Jack, someone's trying to kill you!"

"I know. And that's another reason we don't want you with me. Why I don't want you with me." He dropped his pack and crossed the room back to her, and took her fists into his hands, and uncurled her hands, smoothing out her graceful fingers. He didn't fear her—never had—even though he knew she could kill him with her mind. "You're the only one who knows me and my story."

"I don't know all of it. You've never told me."

"I've told you enough. If something happens to me, then you'll have to tell Purple and you'll have to find the answers, right? We can't let it stop here."

"No." There was a catch in her voice. She swallowed. "I can help you find Winton. I accessed him once over the network—I could do it again."

"Not until I know how he can come after us. He might be buried so deeply that the Emperor has no idea who he is or what he does ... a minor bureaucrat ... someone who knows me from the Sand Wars. Or maybe from Claron. But you, Amber, are to stay out of this until I start getting some answers. There are too many questions now and any one of them could be fatal if you repeat them to the wrong person."

"What about Daku?"

"Daku is dead."

"And you were lucky." Her pupils went wide as her temper flared. "You were lucky I was there!"

"Maybe. All I know for sure is that he wasn't hired because of Claron. He was shocked to know I was involved. Or, he was hired blind, so that he couldn't possibly reveal the true motives if he failed. That would have been the smarter thing to do."

Amber pushed her hand through her hair, but the movement didn't disguise the faint trembling. "Do they think that highly of you? That whatever assassin they send after you might fail?"

He grinned, suddenly. "I don't know. *You* do." He leaned forward, kissed her on the end of her nose, picked up the duffel bag and fled before she could recover. He thought he could hear her thin voice through the walls as he strode away: "Damn you, anyway, Jack Storm!"

A Dominion Knight wore his suit like a second skin. Jack preferred to keep his torso bare, the different clips and leads crimped to his skin kept a little looser and easier that way. The holograph that played over his body and then relayed the movement to the suit like a step-up transformer was bled out now—he had his helmet off and at his feet—but his suit was still quite effective. Cock and point a finger and his gauntlets were weapons. On his back, he could wear a field pack that would make him a devastating force. The only thing that could daunt him was a "red field," a showing of gauges in the red, which would indicate that his power was so drained his suit would become nearly immobile, a burden that could cripple and ultimately destroy the soldier inside.

Red fields were an armor wearer's bane. They had become commonplace on Milos in spite of the solar panels in the helmet that took in a constant, but not great enough, charge. At the moment he had nothing to worry about but the boredom of staying at attention, his gaze flicking back and forth over the audience room of the Emperor of the Triad, Ultimate Commander of the Dominion Forces, Pepys.

He wasn't the only one on duty. Four of them took up the four corners of the room, each gathering his fair share of curious, and in some cases, hostile, glances. Jack delicately set his jaw. It wasn't the stares so much as the comments, as though he were deaf as well as dumb.

A tall, elegant woman, whose silver hair belied the crisp line of her chin and neck, glided past, escorted on the arm of a stout, aloof man. She paused. Her blue-eyed glance examined him thoroughly and her comments were not far different from those he'd been hearing all day.

"So that's one of *them*."

"It would appear, m'dear." Her escort looked about the room, ill at ease with her refined gawking.

"He looks clumsy. I should think Pepys would be better off with a good police robot."

He stroked her gloved hand. "Robots can't keep up with human subtleties, m'dear. Look what happened to our late, lamented emperor. Artificial intelligence simply can't comprehend us. A shiv was stuck through his ribs and pinned him to the throne before the robot perceived a threat." He coughed into his free hand. "An example Pepys doesn't wish to emulate."

"But after all these years. . . ." Her voice trailed off, and then she sniffed. "He's not bad looking, for all that." Curiosity sated, she began moving forward then stopped again. "Good god, Murphy. He's let one of the Walkers in for audience."

"Can't keep 'em out forever, m'dear."

Jack fought to keep his jawline steady. Murphy appeared indifferent to all the cruel stings of fate.

"But he's in line in front of *us*."

Jack did not quite hear Murphy's response as the two pressed forward. He allowed himself the luxury of looking to the front where the aforementioned Walker patiently waited.

Clothed all in blue, loose flowing robe over a miner's jumpsuit, a bulky and crude hand-wrought cross hanging across his chest, the once handsome, now balding and aged man waited. Jack had seen him before. If he wasn't mistaken, this particular Walker had waited for an audience the last five days. Jack had only had substitute duty one of those days, but the Walker prelate wasn't one to overlook. Even if he had no other, patience was definitely this man's virtue. Nor did he seem to take affront that Pepys was about to close the audience down, once again, without his having been received.

"St. Colin of the Blue Wheel," the announcer's voice rang out, and the Walker started imperceptibly, then moved forward to the dais and the Emperor.

Pepys, wiry and compact, of an age with the Walker, made a diffident movement with his hand. The announcer then said, "Audience closed for the day."

The Walker stayed behind as the hall emptied. Jack watched, the rest of his body as immobile as his expression was impassive, his surprise hidden. The Walker would get a private audience then. For a moment, he wished he had his helmet on, with mikes adjusted, just to hear what the two had to say to each other.

The elegant woman dropped a glove as Murphy, visibly upset, urged her to the door. The glove wafted featherlike toward the floor. Jack moved then, fluid and powerful, and caught it before it touched.

His speed and grace brought a startled sound from the woman and Jack allowed himself to smile. A small, but powerful, demonstration of his abilities. He handed her the glove. She snatched it away as though his gauntlet could burn and Murphy's face blanched.

They sped toward the closing doors.

Jack returned to attention. He would not be off duty until Pepys released him.

The emperor came off the dais and sat down at a small side table, where a silver pot steamed. He took his cap off, freeing his fine red hair, and beckoned for the Walker to join him. The two sat, drinking tea and conversing in small talk.

Suddenly Pepys stood up. "You, you, and you, go. Captain Storm, please join us."

Jack picked up his helmet and moved across the now empty, massive audience hall. He was cautious. Walkers were believers, and beliefs could be dangerous.

Pepys looked more irritated than alarmed as he joined them. "St. Colin, Captain Jack Storm, of my newly rejuvenated Dominion Knights."

"Your Grace, I hardly think this is a matter for a tank. Your undercover agents would be far more suited to—"

"You brought this matter to me. I'll handle it in whatever way I think appropriate."

"But these are men of God!"

Jack watched St. Colin sit rigidly in his chair, every fiber of his being containing the outrage which had swept across his face and then abruptly been quelled. "How may I be of service?"

St. Colin looked away, but not before Jack matched his fiery brown gaze. Jack felt a ripple of uneasiness.

"St. Colin has come to me on a matter of some urgency. The Triad tolerates religious freedom, as it does any other, so long as the power struggles do not affect my rule." He smiled thinly. "Although St. Colin would argue that God's rule far precedes me."

"And he would be right, sir," Jack answered.

St. Colin's gaze came back. This time, it had cooled and was taking his measure. The Walker's right hand went to his cross and touched it lightly. "A historian and a scholar," St. Colin said dryly, "hidden beneath that armor."

"Or not so hidden." Pepys finished his tea. "I've seen the captain at work. He came to me highly recommended and graduated at the top of his training class. He will meet your needs, Colin, and with the discretion you require."

"I operate better knowing what I'm up against, Your Highness."

Pepys sputtered a little then, and laughed. "Patience is not one of *his* virtues. Tell him, St. Colin, what you told me."

The sainted one of the Walkers sat back in his chair, his square body tense under his blue robes. He did not look like he had been a saint long. "Where are you from, captain?"

Jack's jaw muscle clenched, then released. If he told the truth, Dorman's Stand, Pepys would be alerted instantly to his unusual background. Dorman's Stand hadn't been habitable by human standards for twenty years. Yet, these two men had an uncanny way of picking out the truth. If they did not, they would not be as high in the power echelon as they were. "An outlying agrarian planet. I'm a farm boy," and he grinned, using one of Amber's favorite dissembling tricks. He wished she were with him now, to distract St. Colin's level brown stare.

"Are you a Christian?"

"My family was."

"Then you're familiar with the Walker sect."

"Somewhat. I know that your primary goal is to verify that your religious figure did indeed walk on other worlds, to 'prepare other rooms in my Father's mansion,' I believe the quote is interpreted."

St. Colin slapped a hand down on the chair arm. "That's it! And we are primarily scholars and archaeologists, no more, no less."

Pepys stirred. "You belittle yourself, sir. Your religious web is woven throughout every planet touched by exploration—and, theoretically, can extend throughout the universe."

They looked at one another. The man who physically ruled the stars, and the other who spiritually could.

"It is to no one's good," St. Colin said tightly, "if we participate in another religious crusade."

Jack's memory flicked back and he thought of the militaristic Walker he'd seen in the bar where Daku ambushed him. He said, "I take it you're worried about a splinter group within your ranks, one more militarily inclined."

"Why, yes." St. Colin looked up rapidly. "But this is a matter for covert intelligence, not for a soldier in—in battle armor."

Jack smiled. "Why not use your own intelligence?"

"Because the fervor is spreading through our ranks like wildfire. The archaeological evidence we seek evades us. The sect grows old and tired and disillusioned. A crusade of conversion, at any cost, appeals to many among us."

Pepys cleared his throat. "Are you interested, Jack?"

"Yes, sir."

"Good. Please consult with the Purple before you go out on your own. Report to me as soon as possible. Dismissed."

As he walked away, the armor making powerful thuds upon the flooring, he thought he heard St. Colin protest faintly, followed by Pepys' comforting murmur, "My dear saint, I think he intends to take the armor off, first." Then, "I hear you have a new site to excavate. Anything interesting?"

"Yes, quite, but getting permission to dig has been nearly impossible. . . ."

The voices faded behind him.

Jack felt that his assignment would be easy. Too easy. The superstitious prickle along his spine kept him alert.

The bartender looked at him as he came in. It was the same one who'd been on duty when Daku had tried to take him out, but he showed no recognition of Jack. Jack went to a booth in the back, where he could keep an eye on the door, and pretended to be drinking.

Three Walkers came in during the course of the evening. None left.

Jack went back to the palace thinking again that it was too easy. He rousted out the Purple.

"I've got the contact site."

"Are they hiring mercenaries or just meeting?"

"My guess is just meeting."

The Purple rubbed his temple soulfully. He sighed. "We've caught them early, then."

"Unless it's a blind."

"I don't think Colin would want to expose his organization like that, unless he were really worried about trouble. Do you want to have the bar staked out?"

Jack licked his lips. "We have to know the meeting night. Computer surveillance would be too obvious and too easily detected and can be too easily bypassed, with the right know-how." An electronic sweep would tip Jack's hand. He had to have live bodies.

"Then do it. Handpick those you want with you, but don't let them know what they're doing. I know a few who would join the Walkers rather than pick them up."

"Right." Jack disconnected the com lines.

Garner licked dry lips. He ran his palm along his spiked haircut and his asphalt dark eyes glittered suspiciously. "You want me to go in without a suit?"

"That's the idea."

He licked his lips again. Then, reluctantly, "I'm nothing without a suit, captain. Nothin'."

"That's not true, Garner. And whatever our differences, I know this is an operation you can do. All you need to do is observe. Later, we'll go in with the suits."

"If there is a later." The man hesitated, then nodded abruptly. "I'll do it, but I'm warning you, Silent Jack. I'll come after you if I have to."

Jack felt an inner warmth. He returned the nod like a salute. "And I'd expect nothing less from you."

The man received the address and time of his assignment stoically, his decision having been made. Jack made a notation on his clipboard after Garner left. Everything was coordinated.

Once he got the information he needed, he would call Purple again. Then Garner would get permission to put on his battle armor and go in.

St. Colin of the Blue Wheel swallowed tightly, his eyelids scraped by the rough blindfold that covered them. He thought bitterly to himself that it must be made from a hairshirt. Even if he lived through the kidnapping, his eyes would be scratched for months.

"Come on, old man."

The ironlike claw at his elbow jerked him forward from the commuter car. He had a moment for a brief thought, like a prayer sent adrift on the wind, that he had hesitated too long in going to Pepys. Then that moment was gone, as his kidnappers shoved him inside a doorway. He went to his knees, stumbling, his mind protesting over having been called an old man, but his body surrendering. A chute opened up as his knees hit and he dropped into the air.

"We don't want him dead. Yet." A new voice bit the air as he hit bottom and lay on his side, gasping. Colin let the owner of the new voice help him to his feet and shuddered slightly as someone ripped off his blindfold. He sucked in his breath and began praying, barely audibly, "The Lord is my shepherd . . ."

The renegades ignored him, for that's what they were—a room full of arrogant, heavily armed renegades who made Colin want to shade his eyes from their too bright stares. He knew what they wanted: a Christian Empire based on the archaeological findings to date and he remembered the horrible crusades in their ancient history that gave him reason to be afraid. The heavy cross swung at his neck, suddenly a tremendous weight. His beleaguered eyes dewed.

Then Colin remembered that he'd been called a saint within his lifetime and straightened, thrusting his shoulders back. "You're fools. Pepys knows of your ambitions. And I won't have you warping the purpose of our order this way."

"You're too late, old man. We've got an assassin within the palace walls right now. By the time Pepys knows what's happening, neither his understanding nor his tin men are going to save him."

Colin swung to his right. In the shadowy storeroom, he saw cases of liquor and other sundries and knew he was below a bar. He also recognized, here and there, a face. One or two even startled him. He made a noise in his throat, then said, "Triad leaders are like sharks' teeth. Pull one and another will spring into his place. Perhaps one not quite so tolerant of your practices. Do you think Pepys was surprised when I told him that we had developed problems?"

"And do you think we're surprised that you went running to him? Now shut up and go sit down in that corner. Your life depends upon it."

Colin turned and looked at the hawk-nosed man who pointed. "Walker, do I know you?"

"Not yet." He bared white teeth in a thin-lipped smile. "But you will. For after this night, we will use you to keep the undecided in line—

you are, after all, sometimes called a saint. And you will tell them what I want you to. We'll be working very closely together."

Colin fought the impulse to squeeze his abused eyes tightly shut. But he met the man's belligerent stare. "You will," he said, "be amazed at what I can do when cornered." He saw the backhanded blow begin, a muscle twitch in the shoulderline of the jumpsuit, a bunching of fabric across the biceps—he had enough time to react and it was his assailant's turn to be surprised as Colin unleashed finely trained reactions.

He caught the wrist, turned it and used the man's weight to flip him, facedown, onto the floor. A prickling of fear gathered between his shoulder blades as he sensed the others gathering to attack him.

"Hold it right there!"

He never heard them coming—silent as shadows, out of the corners of the room. Then the room's walls exploded and more came, through the walls—the Emperor's new guards, massive and impassive, and the renegade Walkers folded quietly, without a fight.

The tall one in white pushed up his face plate like a visor and eyed him. "Are you all right, sir?"

"Yes. Yes, I am." He looked down in surprise to see his right foot planted firmly on his assailant's shoulder, the man's wrist still locked in his hand. He let go and backed up. "You're needed at the palace, Captain Storm."

"I heard. Garner, come with me. The rest of

you, mop up here. We want all as prisoners except this gentleman."

"How did you—how did you get in without being heard?"

Jack smiled, the corners of his eyes wrinkling. "We were here first," he said. "Waiting."

Colin nodded abruptly, and turned away, to give silent thanks that his prayer had been heard.

Jack used the Purple's security code to bypass the systems and bring the hover car down on the roof of the Emperor's wing. He got out and Garner followed him. Garner had his helmet off and tucked under his arm like a second head. His spiked hair had been squashed and was just now fantailing back up, like a once crinkled piece of shrink wrap.

"What are we doing up here?"

"The fastest way in is down." Jack leaned over. He sought, and found, the terraces outside the main ballroom. "Chances are most of the security systems have been circumvented. Anchor here and rappel down to that balcony."

The second man leaned over. Even in the darkness of the night, his face took on a shiny pallor. He quickly donned his helmet.

Jack anchored the rope. He wrapped it around his gauntlets and gave a quick jerk. The test-weight had been chosen to bear up to the weight of the battle armor, but Jack had his doubts. He snapped the rope a couple of times and then mentally shrugged. Once he was over the side, it was all moot anyway. He fashioned the rappel loop and sling and took his position on top of the retaining wall, back to the drop.

He waited until Garner joined him and they pushed off together. The first drop put a sickening feeling in the pit of his stomach until the loop tightened and he slowed himself, then brought his feet up and braked to a stop. Garner bounced, twirled at the end of his line, then scrambled to brace himself, a shuddering twin to Jack. The com came on.

"How much farther?"

Jack looked back and down. He smiled grimly though the other couldn't see it. "Another good drop should do it."

He thought he heard a gulp as he swung his arm back and let the rappel loop him downward.

He hit the balcony a little harder than he wanted, and even though the suit took most of the jolt, he still felt it clear to his kneecaps. Jack moved fast, shrugging out of the rappel sling as fast as he could. Garner plummeted to a stop next to him and began shedding his lines as quickly.

Here the ballroom walls sparkled at them, half-lit even at night. Jack went to the panes of glass in the outside door. He cocked a finger. The laser played a low beam over the glass.

"What're you doing? We can just walk through here."

"Different alarm system. I don't want to set it off if I can help it."

The glass sloughed off under the beam and puddled its way down the door. Jack reached in and gently opened the door. He stepped through, Garner at his heels. He may have set off the silent system, but not the klaxons and that was the main idea. The assassin would have to work his way down this corridor to get to Pepys and Jack wanted the advantage of surprise.

"How do we know if he's gotten past us or not?" Garner asked when Jack told him, as they peered into the outer corridor.

"We don't."

"But then—" Garner's voice staggered to a halt as Jack cut him off.

He swept a quick look over the interior of his helmet. With a side movement, he chinned on his infrared screen and then scanned the hallway. In front of them, minute patches of heat glowed, rapidly fading.

"What are you doing?"

"Check your infrared. And then shut down and stay quiet. I don't know if the assassin's monitoring frequencies or not, but I don't want to chance getting picked up. Follow my lead and if you don't know what you're doing, then stay out of the way." Jack shut off the com. He felt himself frowning. The assassin was getting careless. Maybe, this deep inside the palace, he didn't feel the need for caution. He went after the "footprints."

Garner hesitated, then followed. He watched the man in the white Flexalinks, realizing that Jack moved with a confidence in the battle armor that he could only hope to achieve someday.

He had no chance for another thought as, in front of him, the assassin jumped Jack.

It would take a better mind than his, Garner thought, to describe the mayhem that followed next. Black shadow fought white in the narrow confines of the corridor, dark water trying to drown out a bright sun. No matter how supple and fluid the murderer was, Jack outstepped the kicks, jumps and handblows. The stiffness of the armor flowed away into a grace that made Garner drop his jaw in astonishment.

As the whirling, death-dealing assassin moved, Jack was there to counter it. Wrist to wrist and foot to foot. The assassin seemed unaware he fought armor, not mortal man, and then Garner saw the gleam of instruments in his hands and knew that the assassin could rip Jack open like a can if he wished—if he could just get ahold of Jack.

White divorced black for a second. The assassin crouched, hunched over and panting like a madman. Then, as if realizing he was defeated, he whirled and dove toward the corridor's end, determined to get to the Emperor. Jack cocked his hand and pointed.

With the flare of laser fire, the alarms blasted and the lights came on.

Garner took off his helmet and squinted at Jack in the harsh light of the palace's outer corridor. His nostrils flared at the smell of singed flesh as he stepped over the heap of assassin Jack had just cut down.

"Did you leave enough for Intelligence?"

Jack gave a short nod. He turned away and

took his helmet off, and carried it under his left arm.

Garner skirted the growing puddle of blood. He caught up with Jack. "That was—uh—pretty good."

"Good?"

He flushed. "Well ... thorough. I guess we got the group and the assassin pretty cleanly. I guess the Emperor's going to be pleased with us. I, uh, want to thank you for letting me be in on this."

Jack's eyes glittered. He answered, "No thanks necessary."

"I, ah, also want to apologize for the hard time I gave you in Basic. I guess I was wrong." Garner had taken off his helmet and now examined it as he held it awkwardly between his hands.

"No apology necessary," Jack said crisply. "Consider this a reward for being able to recognize a dangerous man when you see one." He turned on his heels and left as the rapidly marching footsteps of the Intelligence unit coming in to pick up the pieces could be heard swiftly approaching them.

Garner stood, weight balanced slightly on one foot, in wonderment.

"Congratulations, Captain Storm, on a good job." Pepys beamed. He held a 3-D structure in his hands that might have been a game, or a new project, Jack couldn't tell which. The Emperor set the object down. "St. Colin was well pleased, as was I. Intelligence informs me that, had it been necessary to attack the main base, we would have been facing a wall of women and children first." The Emperor shook his head. "A massacre would have taken place." He ran a wiry hand through his frizzled red hair. The electric green eyes held his a moment, and then the Emperor smiled, almost apologetically, in response to something he saw in Jack's face. "Yes, Jack, I'm afraid I used you somewhat. My sources had already reported trouble before Colin came to me. I'm glad that he did. We knew each other years ago and I'd hate to think ill of him now. I thought this was a good opportunity to see what the Guard was made of."

Jack's stomach shifted. He thought of a wall of religious fanatics, women and children, for his suit to wade through. "Thank you, sir," he said stiffly. The collar of his dress uniform scratched at his neck.

Pepys nodded. "At ease, captain. And remember that I owe you one."

Dismissed, Jack turned and left the antechamber. He tasted sourness at the back of his throat. He would collect one of these days.

With that thought in mind, and the realization that he needed someone to talk to, he turned out of the palace and headed for his quarters. Amber hadn't seen them yet. He thought of calling her.

Entertaining that pleasant idea—along with the realization that he would have to make it a special occasion and Amber cared little for budgets—he made his way to his private quarters.

The battle armor was hanging inside, cleaned and powered after the last encounter. It tugged at him now, calling for him with thoughts of victory and invincibility. Jack shrugged the call aside. He was still in command of the suit, but he should probably ask Amber for additional reinforcement. He punched the handlock and pushed his door open. As he crossed the doorway, he heard an almost imperceptible snap and then a rush of air. He panicked.

Jack reeled and hit the floor face first.

PART II

CHAPTER 4

Sand. Everywhere, the rolling, waving hills of sand. Jack ran his tongue over his teeth, feeling the grit across his enamel. Intelligence reports said that a microbe inhabited the sand, a tiny, living being that Thraks fed on the way whales did plankton from the ocean. He didn't know about that, but he did know about chiggers, and the sand affected him the same way once he took the suit off.

He straightened, feeling naked without his armor, and looked out over the dunes. He shouldn't be here. He knew that. And it was cold, very cold, so that with every step he took, he broke a crust of ice over the sand, sending it crackling away from his boots.

He was alone and unarmored, fighting a war he knew had long since ended. Jack scrubbed at his face. The corners of his eyes were crusted as though he'd been asleep.

Sleep. His heart made a thump in his chest. He looked at his hands and saw they were whole again, and knew a second of blind panic. He was dreaming—he'd been locked into cold sleep again.

And it was a dream from which he could not wake himself.

"Lieutenant!" A heavy hand pounded his shoulder. "Repair says th' suits are ready to go."

Jack knew the voice of his sergeant. Reality slipped away from his grasp as he was locked into repeating the last fateful days of his battle on Milos. "All right, sarge. Tell 'em to suit up. We've been ordered to make a drop." Was that what he'd said? Exactly? Would he get it right this time? Or could he skew it around and change it—Jack swung around.

Staging met his eyesight, with his platoon standing around in various levels of readiness. His sergeant pushed a laser rifle into his hands and said, "Need any help, lieutenant?"

"No. No thanks, sarge." Jack turned away, bile acrid in his throat. His suit waited for him, swaying on an equipment rack. He said nothing more, but inside he was screaming. He was caught in an endless loop of memories in which there was no glory and no victory.

"You don't have to do it. They can't make you." Amber materialized next to him, swinging her tawny mane of hair with customary defiance.

"I'm locked in."

"Aw, c'mon, farm boy. You know better than that. The two of us can do anything together. I got the street smarts and you're the white knight—remember?" She looked at him with pretended wide-eyed innocence. "You mow 'em down and I'll pick their pockets, right?"

Jack blinked. Thraks didn't have pockets. He reached out to touch her shoulder and she crumbled into a pile of beige and pink sand. He leaned over and picked up a handful, letting it run out of his fingers. Unlike everything else here, the sand that had been Amber was warm. At his back, the platoon kidded each other with warm obscenities while they suited up. Then, there was silence as Jack stood.

A growl pierced the air. It set the hair on Jack's neck on end. He forced himself to turn around.

They stood in rows like gaming pieces upended in the sand, in armor that might as well be empty for all the animation they showed. The face plates were screened, reflecting a charcoal emptiness back at him. Jack forced a swallow down a dry, constricted throat. He was afraid, deathly afraid, because he knew what was going to happen next. "Sarge? Sarge!"

The armor groaned. It was a sound that came from deep in the earth under their boots, vibrating upward through stone layers and sand. Jack shuddered to hear it. He felt sweat beading his brow. He needed to get into his own armor, for protection and power, but he stood, rooted.

As Knights, they'd painted insignia on their chests. Family logos, symbols, irreverent gestures. The armor facing him represented men he'd trained with and led and he knew every beige, white, black, khaki, and brown Flexalinked man he faced.

But these were no longer men. Jack brushed the back of his hand across his forehead, smearing the sweat, and heard the noise of the armor tearing apart, as the beast within burst out.

Huge. Bigger than the armor, cloaked in shreds of bone and flesh that had once been human, the great gray-green reptile burst out. White teeth flashed and red eyes burned, and a frill went up as the berserker charged him.

Jack closed his eyes and screamed, but the sound never left his throat.

He was alone, walking the sand dunes of Milos, where grass and a forest had once grown. The Thrakian sands crunched under his feet like glass because it was cold, terribly cold, and he knew he'd been trapped in cold sleep again.

Amber felt chilled by the night air as the Purple's hard hand closed over her elbow, guiding her through the compound. She'd had time enough to throw a robe on, but her feet were bare. She asked no more questions, because she knew that he wouldn't answer any more than he already had. All she knew was that something had happened to Jack.

She stumbled across a rough tile and stifled the pain in her throat. The Purple was tense and angry and she wondered if he blamed her for whatever had happened.

They reached the officer's quarters, deep inside the Emperor's private grounds. Light beaconed across the walkway, spilling out from an open door. She saw uniformed men standing around inside ... other bodyguards and, her lips thinned, World Police. She had little regard for the intelligence squad. She'd have to mind her manners. Jack would expect it of her.

But, to her relief, she saw no sprawled corpse on the flooring as the Purple guided her in.

The Guard straightened and snapped out a salute. The Purple returned it. "Anything definite?"

"Just this, sir." One of the intelligence officers held out a tiny plastic capsule. "We found it rigged just inside the overhead venting."

"What was in it?"

Amber stared at the capsule pinched between the Purple's fingers. Gas. Potent, too, from the size of the capsule.

"As near as we can tell, it wasn't toxic. Knockout, probably. Lab reports will tell us more."

Her gaze skimmed the room. There were no signs of a struggle. Bogie stood on a rack in the corner gleaming in the artificial light. She'd wait until the room had been emptied, then see if the suit had sensed anything. Its growing sentience flickered in and out of awareness, usually only alive if Jack occupied the armor . . . but she was willing to try anything, even if it meant coping with Bogie's belligerence.

"Have we had a ransom call?"

"No, sir. Not yet."

The Purple looked down at Amber. "I think it's safe to assume that Jack is still alive, or he wouldn't have been taken alive. We'll find out why whenever they want us to know."

She looked up. "And that's it? That's all you're going to do?"

"We'll have to examine the sentry tapes, see if our cameras recorded anything."

The World Police officer said stiffly, "It's already been done, sir. There's no record of any breaking or entering. No one was in these premises except for the captain."

Amber snorted. She looked around. Chances were the tapes had been altered, or wiped, or the cameras circumvented. Any amateur could do as much. She wasn't impressed.

The Purple dismissed the officers. He stood in the doorway. "You can't stay. This is a high security area."

She flopped down in an armchair. "You mean it *was* a high security area. Just for a little while. I know him better than anyone. There might be something here we've overlooked. Maybe the gas didn't get him. Maybe he's gone out after someone."

The silver-haired man looked at her. His deep brown eyes accented his tanned face. The expression wasn't the humorous expression she remembered. He looked, she reflected, worried. "All right. I'll give you an hour or two, but then call for an escort and go home, all right?"

Amber nodded. "All right." She swiveled the chair around as the front door closed. She looked at Bogie.

His hands burned and his left foot was in agony. Jack writhed in the darkness that surrounded him.

"Careful there. This man's had frostbite injuries before . . . look at the amputations. Couple of toes here and a finger there."

"Cold sleep?"

"I doubt it. Anyone that cold generally doesn't wake up."

Jack struggled. He could feel hands roaming over him. He swam through the blackness and held his breath, trying to break surface.

"Breathing's irregular."

"He's coming out of it, doctor. It's the drowning syndrome."

Voices washed over him fuzzily.

"All right then. Watch him. Keep an eye on the monitor. We could still lose this one to defib. I don't like the reaction."

"Yes, sir."

Jack twisted, then relaxed, as a warm sheet covered his body. He began to shiver violently, out of control, his teeth chattering. He still couldn't get his eyes open, but he clenched his teeth.

"Take it easy." The woman's low voice soothed him. He felt the weight of another thermal blanket being draped over him.

"You . . . found me."

"Found you? No, you've been right here, berthed with everyone else. Just lie back until you're warmed. You've had a tough time coming out of it."

Jack felt the blankets being tucked in. He tried to move a hand and found it strapped down. "Lost. We've been lost." His eyelids flickered. He'd been lost for seventeen years, asleep, and now was found again. He relaxed as the shivering abated. He was awake again, found again. Claron and rangering would be awaiting him. He'd dreamed the firestorm. Life would be good and green again. Everything was fine. Nothing would go wrong this time.

"Take it easy, Amber. We've done all we can."

She paced the office, her strides carrying her ceaselessly back and forth. "It's been a month. He's either dead or off planet."

"I think if he was dead, we'd know it. If it had been Rolf or anyone else taking revenge, the body would have been left where we could find it. You know that."

"Then he's off planet."

"Where we can't trace him." The Purple looked at her impassively. "The same freedoms that Jack treasured—not being in the master system, not having a wrist chip for ID—they're keeping us from tracing him now. There's no record of Jack anywhere."

She spun to a halt. "He's got to be somewhere! He wouldn't just leave the suit behind. Would you?"

"No," answered the Purple slowly. "But neither of us really knows that much about Jack."

"I know that he'd tell me where he was if he could!" She felt a hot wetness spring up in her eyes. Dammit! She never cried. Now here she was, about ready to cry over Jack again, for the second time in weeks. She blinked fiercely. "He's not dead. I'd know if he was."

The Purple locked gazes with her and she thought suddenly, *he knows more than he's told me*. He broke the stare and looked down at his desk. Amber's intuition flooded her. She knew Jack would not have discussed her abilities with the Purple and she licked her lips, suddenly apprehensive.

The commander looked up then. "We think he's been taken, Amber. Slave labor, maybe, by someone with an old grudge. It might be someone from our mercenary background, I'm not sure. That's all I can tell you." He rubbed at his temple with slim, elegant fingers. "I'll call you if I can find out anything else."

Amber went to the door. "All right." She left, without the slightest compunction over the severe headache she'd given the man by psychically encouraging him to talk to her. She'd do anything to find Jack.

He dreamed of Claron. The planet was his, virgin and untamed, a world of lush green forests and plains, new jagged purple mountains and white untouched snowcaps. He could skim for weeks without sign of human habitation. He could sense the touch, taste and smell of the planet.

Until he dreamed the firestorm. He felt the vibration and thrum, the eardrum beating noise of warships breaking into the stratosphere. He remembered leaving his quarters and seeing the sky burn. He remembered getting into his armor and finding the stargate, being knocked through by the bombs bursting around him, drifting for days on the other side, until he was finally found. And it was in the whirl of black velvet deep space that he lost himself. In a blast of fever, he lost what few memories he'd been left.

* * *

"Jeeee-zus Christ. Doesn't this guy ever do anything but moan?"

"Some kind of allergic reaction to cold sleep. Quit your bitching and deal. You gonna ante up or what?"

"If he's that sick, they shoulda left him in sick bay."

"Ante up, Stash!"

"All right, mate, all right."

He opened his eyes. The dull orange glow of night lighting met his sight. The vibration and thrum of his dreams still wrapped around him. Self-identity swam out of reach. He let it go, finding it easier to identify his surroundings. He was shipboard. He lay quietly. His hands were loosely strapped to his sides. The stale smell of too many bodies packed into close quarters and the smoke of drugsticks reached him. He turned his head. Most of the berths were occupied by forms, still and blanketed like himself. Soft snoring rumbled through the air. What was happening to him?

The snap of cards punctuated the silence. The semblance of normality drew him like a magnet. He saw two figures hunched over a small table in the aisleway of the bay. The blue-gray smoke of drugsticks wavered over them. They wore nondescript, faded brown jumpsuits and both men looked like they'd seen better days. The young one faced him, but his attention was fixed on the bits of plastic clenched in his hands. His hair was butcher cut, any which way, and his eyes looked like hard flints in his sharp-planed face. He wasn't beautiful and, as the sick man watched him palm a card, his playing partner momentarily distracted, he wasn't honest, either.

His playing partner made a disgusted noise. He threw his hand in, saying, "I'd have better luck with Thraks droppings."

The young man grinned, a vicious expression. "Shut up and deal."

"I'm tired. Let's hit the bunks."

"Forget it! You owe me. All we've got tomorrow is orientation. Shit. You and I've mined before. What do they expect from us?" The man leaned forward. "I tell you what I'm going to do. I'm going to break contract. They 'aven't built a contract yet that can hold me."

The old man made a sucking noise through broken teeth. "You'd better watch your step, Stash. This place is different. You're getting paid good money for your contract."

"Maybe." Stash looked around briefly, overlooking the berths. "But there's bodies here that didn't volunteer to be here. I figure there's money to be made getting them out." He wove his hands together and turned them inside out to pop his knuckles. "I'm not one to avoid making money if I have to."

As the cards snapped in the deal, a fuzzy voice yelled out, "Hey, you two! It's downtime, okay?"

"Yeah, yeah," Stash returned. He stood up. "You owe me, Boggs." His gaze brushed over the berths again and this time, the watcher had the uneasy feeling his gaze was met. Stash turned away and climbed into one of the stacks of berths, pulled the freefall webbing and a blanket over him and was asleep in a matter of seconds.

The sick man settled back onto his bunk. A wave of dizziness washed over him, and reality blended into hallucination. Where was he, and when? He anchored onto the name and face of Stash. A feeling tickled at the back of his mind. He felt a familiarity there. If he needed help getting out, Stash would be the name to remember. He clutched to it like a drowning man as he went under again.

He awoke drenched with sweat, and with the feeling someone was watching him. He was right. The man named Stash squatted at the foot of the berth, intently reading the plasticard file stored there. He looked up. "Awake, eh, mate? We're alone. Th' others have gone to chow down. Want some help out? The nurse said your ropes could come off if you wanted, long as you acted sane." The flint dark eyes twinkled sardonically. "But which of us ain't a little crazy, eh?"

He swallowed and weakly lifted his hands. "Please . . . take them off."

Stash moved quickly. "Good enough. You want to try eating?"

He thought about it and then, quickly, shook his head.

Stash took a ration card from the plasticard envelope, saying, "Then you don't mind if I help myself. Payment, like, for untying you. A little extra tuck goes down good now and then." The scarred eyebrow quirked. "What's your name, mate?"

He shook his head, mouth too dry to talk.

Stash scrubbed a hand through his butcher-cut dark hair. "Hypothermia fever is what you had. It's tough. I've seen it before. Fella didn't even know his name when he woke up." Stash fingered the envelope. "You got ration cards from last shift you'll never catch up on. Make you a deal. I'll read you your file for two of them."

He wet his chapped lips and croaked, "Deal."

Stash beamed triumphantly. He took the chits out. "Be back later, mate. Get your rest and mind you don't fall out of the berth or th' nurse'll have my hide. I've got plans for her to have a part o' me, but me hide's not what I had in mind."

The sleeper closed his eyes, weary again.

"Let's see here. File says you're Jack Storm, twenty-four. You signed on as construction or mining laborer. Single," and Stash broke his concentration at this to put in, "ain't we all, mate?"

"Go on." The name meant little, but he realized with a sinking heart what his situation was now. He was no more than a contracted slave. Jack. He rolled that around a little. He was somewhat comfortable with it.

Stash cleared his throat. "You ran an electronics store in the Outward Bounds. Went belly-up and sold out to pay off your debts. Standard education. That's about it."

"Relatives?"

"None living." Stash dropped the plasticard

file back into its envelope. "Utterly undistin-
guished, like the rest of us. You fit in, Jack me
boy."

"Yes. I guess I do." Jack closed his eyes wearily. He'd been rousted out for breakfast and an
exercise period, his legs as wobbly under him as
a newborn foal's. He wondered blackly how he
could know about contract labor and freight
cruisers and newborn foals and still not quite
grasp his own sense of self. Without opening an
eye, he said, "Thanks, Stash. But put that ration
card back. I paid you yesterday."

The man cleared his throat and the plasticard
file rustled a little. "So you did, so you did. And
from the looks of you, you'll be needing it. Get
your rest, mate. You'll be needing that, too."

"All right, you slag heaps. Hit the decks. I
want a full turnout this morning."

Jack staggered up, the harsh tones of a D.I.
ringing in his ears. He found fresh red marks on
his wrists and, rubbing them, fell into line. His
legs decided to hold him this time. He was un-
washed and unshaven and the rough brown
jumpsuit, not made to his size, bound him. General issue, he thought, shrugging uncomfortably.
He rubbed shoulders as they lined up in the
aisle.

A short, squat bull of a man swaggered through.
He held up a hand of chips. "I'm your foreman.
I've got your labor contracts and past work records right here. I want you to know, we'll put
up with no slackers. You're getting paid good

money to work Lasertown. You'll be rightside up when your contract's done."

Uncomprehending, Jack listened. He rubbed his face once, as if clearing his sight could clear his hearing. The sights and sounds bled over, then faded away. He remembered hearing the hiss of gas. . . .

He straightened.

"We'll be hitting dirtside soon. I want you sorted into work groups, ready to go. As I call your name, fall out and follow me."

Jack clenched his jaw. He'd recognized the name of Lasertown with a jolt that hadn't even come when Stash read him his. He was as good as enslaved, and as good as dead, for a dead moon mining community had its own laws of survival. Jack couldn't work a job he didn't remember being trained for. Fellow workers wouldn't tolerate a man who couldn't work . . . their existence depended on it. He'd be left alive for a short while but his shortcomings would be exposed soon enough. All someone had to do was cut his line and set him adrift, or bring a mountain of rock down on his head, or puncture the suit with a slow leak.

The foreman looked around expectantly as if waiting to hear a protest. He got none. A voice from the back of the bay called out, "Come on, Bull, read the bad news." He grinned and swaggered to the front of the bay and stood by the bulkhead. He took out a microfiche reader and squinted at the first contract.

"Perez, John. Wiring and Cable. Fall in."

"Stockton, Marty. Wiring and Cable."

Jack stood, waiting for his name. He looked across the aisle and saw the sardonic expression of the man across from him. He frowned.

"What you lookin' at, pretty boy?" Stash jibed at him.

Jack bared his teeth. "You." He hadn't seen his greedy benefactor for a day or so.

Stash smiled back. They talked quietly so as not to disturb the bullhorn voice of the foreman. "You know you going to be that sick when you signed up?"

Jack shook his head and countered, "What difference does it make to you? You wanna hold my hand?"

Stash made a rude noise and Jack finished, "I didn't think so. What I do is my business."

"Yeah? Well, if you want out, that's my business."

"First things first," Jack answered. "I've got to live that long."

"Oh, yeah? Memory bank still down?"

"Maybe. And I've got a feeling it could be fatal."

"You could be right, mate. Follow my lead." Stash shut up as abruptly as he'd spoken, and fastened his attention in the direction of the foreman.

The line of workers thinned out, and they had to crowd closer to hear the foreman over the clamor of laborers gathering their belongings and moving out. The rumble of the ship as it moved into a disintegrating orbit grew louder.

Stash grabbed his duffel. Jack found a limp,

nearly empty duffel tucked at the foot of his berth and shouldered it. Stash eyed the bag.

"Travel light."

"I've got all I need."

"Right. That's what they all say." Stash grinned again as the foreman called out, "Grue, Delman. Welding."

"That's me," he said, and shouldered past. He yelled out to the foreman, "Call me Stash."

"Just get in line."

The crowd was thinned down to a double handful of men. Jack felt uneasy.

"Storm, Jack. Demolition."

The word jolted him. The most exacting and dangerous job in mining. He was as good as dead. A wiry and leathery old man next to him said, "Demolition? Never heard of you."

Jack looked at him. The veterans knew the men in their field. Words dried in his mouth.

Stash leaned over the foreman and bumped the microfiche reader. "Hey, Bull. That says welder. You got lint on your lenses. C'mon, Jack."

The foreman looked up and set his long jowls. "All right, Stash. Get him out of here."

Jack shouldered his way through, feeling sweat trickling down his ribs, and a faint reprieve. Stash gave him a look as they ducked to go through the bulkhead. "You owe me," he said softly.

Jack had no doubt that he did and that Stash wouldn't hesitate about collecting.

CHAPTER 5

Amber had not figured to be back on the streets again. She sat in the corner of the commuter car as it three-wheeled across the border that separated Malthen proper from the underbelly of Malthen—the part of the world system that operated outside the law and under laws of its own. She stretched a leg out to check the power blade sheathed along the outside of her right ankle. A visor at the front of the car reflected her image back at her: collected, unremarkable, professional. She could have gone as she did when she followed Jack, but she wanted no attention or trouble here. Dressed as she was now, with weapons discreetly blurring the outlines of her jumpsuit, no one was likely to bother her. Professional assassins weren't hassled, even on the lawless side.

She wouldn't even be noticed, if she played the part well, staying outside the security camera angles that panned the street for the Sweeps and drawing no attention to herself. And, within her costuming, there was no reason to remember her even if she should be encountered. She needed that now, more than ever, because the person she sought, if she was right, would turn and run the moment he knew she was back in South Malthen.

It hadn't been that many months since she'd been found by Jack, but it was the same as a lifetime ago to her. She'd shed her old life like a worn-out garment. Even cleaned and patched up, it felt slimy to pick up and wear again. She intended to return home as soon as possible.

If she still had a home. Home, by Amber's definition, wasn't so much a place as a state of being. Jack's disappearance had seriously disrupted all of that for her. For herself, as well as Jack, she had to find him.

The commuter car braked. She leaned forward and, with a little fine-tuning, convinced the car's circuitry to carry her around the block to a different, unstored, destination. She got out and looked around. She leaned back in long enough to log a fake destination call and the car lurched away from the curb as soon as she pulled the probe away. With a grim smile, Amber put away her tool and stored it. Another pat to be sure the blade was where she could pull it quickly. Ordinary assassin she was not, but she would have been stupid to have been unafraid.

She couldn't remember not being on the streets. Rolf had given her free rein, teaching her how to steal and letting her keep the rewards until she was good enough to steal more than fruits or toys. He'd educated her and treated her well enough—she was lucky, she knew, that he'd never abused her, for most of the children on the streets were used for a multitude of purposes. Now she knew it was not because of any goodness on Rolf's behalf. Buried in her memories was a moment when he had tried and she'd struck back, mentally, disabling her guardian for days. When he'd regained all his faculties, he set out not to punish her but to mine the unexpected gold he'd found.

He'd sold her abilities to an unknown purchaser and then set about teaching her, honing her, to be a weapon the likes of which few could ever hope to own. He'd taught her meditation, to increase her concentration and control. He'd sublimated her ability almost immediately so that Amber herself was unaware of what he was teaching her to do. She only knew that she had it a little easier as a thief on the streets than most did—and that prostitution was not required of her, only the dry hustle, entreating a john and then robbing rather than submitting.

Twice, such scams had gone wrong. Both times, she'd remembered little of what happened—only waking next to a corpse. Rolf had told her she'd killed the john, but she had doubted that, knowing that any time Rolf could sink a hook into her, he would do so. She privately thought that Rolf had killed the unruly clients, then arranged the evidence so that it would appear she had done so . . . to mire her ever deeper in his debt. So she continued to think until Jack found her, and she'd been forced to throw in her lot with the injured man. He'd had enemies of his own and then Rolf had turned on her and she'd been forced to run. It was then she'd found out the truth: she could kill—and had killed—with her mind.

And a future target was sublimated somewhere deep within, awaiting the right buzzword to set it off.

She needed Jack to protect her from herself. She *had* to find him.

Not that Jack's enemies would be any easier to deal with. He told her little, operating on the assumption that the less she knew, the less danger she would be exposed to by associating with him. Amber understood the logic and though she argued with it from time to time, those arguments were rare. She'd gleaned more from Jack than he knew, anyhow. Storm came from a different culture and background. Dissembling brought a faint blush to his plain, high-boned face, and a pained look to his light blue eyes. An out and out lie nearly broke his tongue.

Amber looked up at the bar's entrance. She entered diffidently, on the fine edges of the camera's eyeview of the place. Any image she left behind would be fleeting, blurred, shadowy. She'd not be recognized. She slipped into the corner quickly, threw her head up and looked around. She'd no hope of catching Ballard before he saw her—but she had every hope of getting him before he could get out of the bar, and he'd bolt, she'd stake everything on it!

There was a scuffling in the far corner. Amber hurtled over a table, ran across the chair and booth backs, and leaped, colliding with the man making a run for the back door. They hit with a grunt and rolled onto the floor. She dug her fingers into his scalp and hung on as he shook and gave a dull roar of anger. Wrapping herself around his torso she hissed into his ear, "I'm dressed as an assassin and there won't be anyone in here too surprised if I stick a knife in your eye, so don't tempt me!"

Ballard growled and threw her off. Amber rolled as she hit the floor and threw a psychic bolt at him, her eyes narrowing and temple throbbing as she fought to contain her power.

The spacer, on his feet and halfway out the rear exit, reeled back. He sank to his knees and cradled his head in his hands. He forced out, "Stop it!"

Amber sat up. "Talk to me."

Ballard pulled himself into an empty booth. She slid in opposite him. The man looked up— one eye bloodshot, the other an empty golden grill. His dark ringlets of hair showed flecks of gray. He was sweating. She passed along a napkin.

"What do you want? I thought you were off the streets."

"I am." She felt her chin go up and out.

"What the hell did you do to me?"

She shrugged. "A little trick. A dart in the right place. You'll be all right in an hour or so." Let him think she'd needled him. She didn't need Ballard knowing any of her secrets. Jack was the only person she trusted with those. "I'm not here for old times' sake. What do you know about Jack?"

The tan Ballard liked to affect blanched. He

blinked, but the gold screen replacing his other eye continued to observe her. "I don't know anything."

"You know he was a survivor of the Sand Wars."

Ballard hissed her silent. He massaged the back of his neck. "That's enough to get us all killed. He survived and I deserted. We're both on borrowed time."

Amber flexed her wrist and brought out a paper thin throwing blade. "What's happened to him?"

The spacer looked at her, his one good eye wild. "What do you mean?"

She aimed the knife and he said, "He was picked up."

"What do you mean?"

"He was supposed to have been killed, but he was chilled and shipped out instead. The original shipper was killed for his error. I don't know where he went. Rumor is, he won't be coming back anyway."

Amber felt cold inside herself. "Contract labor?"

"Probably." Ballard crumbled the paper napkin in his hand, then opened it up and wiped his sweating forehead a second time. "Some free advice. Stay out of this, Amber."

"Was it Rolf?"

"Your pimp's got no love lost for the guy, but he's been clean. It was someone big—much bigger. We're both dead if we meddle."

Amber showed her teeth and lifted the knife a little higher. "Some of us are dead anyhow."

"Listen to me! Use your street savvy. I would have sent word to you if I could. I got respect for Jack Storm. The man is a true Knight. He knows what it means to wear the armor ... fight the "Pure" war. There's no one like him alive today ... maybe one or two others, I don't know for sure. I'd have helped if I could!"

The knife point glittered before his last human eye. Ballard blinked frantically. "I'm telling you the truth. I ... keep track of Jack, just to see what he's doing. No one came to me—no one squealed—they didn't have to. Whoever had him swept in already knew who and what he was—it was just a matter of finding out where."

Amber settled back a little. She resheathed the knife in her wrist sleeve. She thought Ballard was telling her the truth. "All right," she said, relenting. Now she'd have to track down the contract labor shipments. And Jack in cold sleep—she shivered. It might drive him over the edge to be trapped like that again. "I need a chip, Ballard. Make it a good one. I don't want to be picked up for using a terminated account or wearing a false chip."

Ballard smiled weakly. He pulled out his wallet after checking to see that they were still off camera. The bartender looked briefly his way, then discreetly looked away. Ballard tapped out a chip. It dropped onto the table, barely the size of one of her fingernails.

"Take this one. It belongs to the Duchess."

Amber's hand hovered over it briefly. She'd clawed her way out of South Malthen to live where chip implants weren't necessary to buy goods, provide ID, trace movements, or just to live. She picked it up. Ballard taped it to the inside of her wrist with flesh colored tape. Now, if the monitors picked her up, she'd be riding the Duchess' account.

Amber smiled herself. She'd always wanted to be an interplanetary jewel thief. "What'll I owe you?"

"Nothing. The Duchess was needin' an alibi anyhow. She asked me to find someone to wear it around for a few months. I consider this a favor for letting me stay alive."

She laughed at his ironic tone. Amber stood up. "See you around, Ballard. I'll send the chip back, one way or another."

"Do that." Without being told to, Ballard stayed very still and quiet in the booth as she left. His gold screen eye followed her, unwinking, and very unsympathetic.

CHAPTER 6

"You'd be a hard man to sneak up on now, wouldn't you?" Stash said, from the dawning corner of the bay. The artificial night of the lighting system faded slowly, leaving him a half-illuminated silhouette.

Jack lifted his head from the bunk. "Maybe. What do you want?"

"Wouldn't you like to know? You wake up four, five times a night, you know that?"

His head ached, but he answered, "I have some idea of it."

"How come?"

"I like to keep an eye on you."

Stash bared his teeth in a grin. "Really? I'm flattered."

Jack swung his feet around and sat up, finally placing the man's faint accent. New Aussie or maybe Cockney. Stash stood braced in the portal, a deepsuit in his hands. "What's that for?"

"I've come to give you lessons, mate."

"It'll wait until after landing."

Stash's teeth-baring smile widened to a grin.

"Not hardly. From what I've heard around here, landings are tough. Maybe not even possible."

The hair rose on the back of Jack's neck. Definitely not a good sign. He shook off the last of his bad dreams, of cold sleep and betrayal. "What do you hear?"

The ship shuddered even as Stash straightened up, and he looked around, his grin suddenly gone.

"Lasertown's got an embargo, y'might say. It's a bit difficult gettin' in and out."

"Whose?"

"Thraks."

In the stifling closeness of the bay, Jack stepped over the bodies of sleeping workers and felt chilled. He met Stash at the bay and took the heavy, sagging deepsuit from him. He closed the bulkhead behind him. They stood in the shop and Stash pulled another suit off its rack.

"What do you mean, Thraks?"

The man shrugged. "That's what I'm told. It's not an official violation of the Treaty or anything, so the Triad looks the other way. It's got something to do with trade and mineral rights. Minerals. Th' only thing Lasertown's good for. Anyhow, word around here has it that when we start our spin in, we got a better chance of making it if we got suits on. That way, if the captain gets careless and we gets a hole blown in the side real sudden, we don't get depressurized. Right, mate?"

"Right," Jack mumbled. He opened the sealing seam and looked into the suit. The palms of his hands itched. He wanted his memory back.

He survived better if he stayed angry, rather than scared.

"Lost a finger there?"

It hadn't really been a question, but Jack looked up into Stash's face. The other looked vaguely interested. "Yes."

"Fight?"

"Frostbite. I got left in cold storage too long, once." He'd said it sarcastically, but once said, the hearing of it jolted him. Had he been? It didn't seem probable, but—

Stash interrupted his thoughts. "No kidding? Well, you won't need that one for the welding gloves, anyway. Okay, this is how it's done. You'll be getting insulating socks. Wear them. Step in, but leave the suit collapsed on the floor like this so you can hook up."

Jack watched, bemused that Stash took it for granted he'd had no experience with a deepsuit before, and wondering what angle the man had, for it was crystal clear that everything Stash did had a price on it. But the man had vouched for him as a welder, so maybe it was just as well he had his own back protected, too.

"These are the catch bags. We're in these suits twelve, fourteen hours a day, so keep them and yourself clean. And if you get an infection or anything—even the tiniest itch—get to Med Bay. Otherwise, you might have things fallin' off of you and we wouldn't want that now, would we, mate?"

Jack didn't answer, but continued to suit up as Stash babbled on. The suit felt flimsy, spineless, for all it was made from layers of a tough fabric. Once on, it was, at the same time, much bulkier and much flimsier than it looked. He ran a hand down his flank.

There was no power in this suit. It was a burden, hanging from his shoulders, pulling down the length of his body. If he moved, flexed, the suit hampered it. It felt both eerily wrong and right, warring with his memories.

Jack didn't like the feel of it.

Stash seemed to sense that. He paused, helmet in hand. "It's not much, but it'll keep you alive."

That, ultimately, was what counted. He caught the helmet Stash threw at him. "What's in this for you, mate?" he said.

Stash did a double take, then smiled widely at the mocking accent. "Why, mate," he answered. "Money, of course." He laughed as he turned and waded the length of the shop bay, and disappeared through the bulkhead.

Jack hesitated a few moments, afraid to follow him, and gritted his teeth in disgust at the turmoil boiling in his stomach. He looked at the helmet in his hands and longed to crush it between his palms. How long had he been this disoriented? Thoughts rushed through his mind like an icy wind. What the hell had happened to him? Where the hell had he come from and how long had he been gone? He could have been chilled down and kept for years, maybe, before being shipped out. He looked after Stash. He couldn't pin it down, but the man's face nagged at him. He rubbed the battered face plate of the old deepsuit thoughtfully.

"Nasty being, that Stash is," sounded a voice behind him. "Been partnering with him long?"

Jack turned. A small, wiry man, with hooked nose and gray hairs that peeked out of his nostrils, watched him. The man had more hair in his ears and his nostrils than he had on his head. He recognized Stash's much cheated against cardplayer.

"I'm Boggs. Alfredo Boggs." The s whispered a little through broken teeth.

"Jack Storm. I'm not partnering with Stash. I just . . . know him."

The wiry man spit into a corner of the shop bay. "Best to keep it that way."

"He cheats you at cards," Jack said patiently.

"That he does. And he knows I know it. I'd rather play with a known cheat than one that sneaks up on you. Get your throat cut that way." Boggs eyed Jack with watery hazel eyes.

He shrugged. He put the helmet back on a hook and began to unsuit. A sudden familiarity swept him. His eyes blurred.

Boggs crossed his arms as he watched Jack brightly. "Storm. Unusual name, that is."

"It goes back to the first crossing," Jack said without thinking. "Amerind, the family told me." It came out, unconsciously and so quickly he scarcely knew where it had come from and it felt *right*. It was him. Part of the him he'd lost.

Boggs helped him drag the suit to a rack and hang it up. "Been welding long?"

"Not very."

"We all had in mind that none of us had heard of you until Stash spoke up."

Jack looked down at Alfredo Boggs. The man was past middle-aged prime and tough as an old rat. "Tell you what, Pops. You didn't get that old working with a crew that was green or stupid. I'm not that green and I'm definitely not stupid."

Boggs seemed unmoved, though his hazel eyes blinked. "We'll see about that," he responded. "We'll see about it."

The sleeping bay was filled with sour smelling, tense bodies, strapped to their bunks as the intercom buzzed on. "Thirty seconds to descent pattern. All hands secure themselves. Thirty seconds . . ."

The ship bumped. Jack felt the jolt through his bones. Several feet away, in an under bunk, a voice swore. He recognized Alfredo Boggs' rusty tones.

"Jesus. We're hit already."

A rustling went through the barracks. Jack had a mental image of a stampede for the deep-suits in the other bay. "No, that's not it. That's just spin off turbulence. Hang in there, Pops." No sooner had he finished speaking than the ship dodged abruptly as though they had all fallen off a ledge.

Someone else muttered, "Evasive pattern. We've got a son-of-a-bitch Bug on our tail."

Thraks. Gray silence hung in the bay. There was a groan as the ship cut rapidly in another direction and for a brief second, they all hung facedown from their bunks, straps cutting into their bodies.

90

As quickly, they righted.

Jack had to give the pilot credit. He flew as good an evasive pattern as any warship Jack had ever been on. Not that that made it any easier for his stomach to take. He shut his eyes briefly and created a center of gravity for himself. His thoughts whirled. He knew battle cruisers. Somehow, he knew. Another groan cut through the silence. Jack clenched the handholds. Then the ship bucked. It skipped, steadied, then hiccoughed again. He recognized the movement.

"Now you can start sweating, Pops. We're being fired at." The ship sheared off suddenly. Jack bit his lip.

Cold sweat dotted his forehead. The ship twirled. He felt the bump, bump, bump of blasts shaking the freighter. Jack tore off his belt. He got to his feet.

Bump. Jack fell with a thud, the edge of the bunk slamming into his head. Crimson exploded and he reeled back, sick with pain. A berthmate reached out and grabbed his arm, keeping Jack in place on the floor as the freighter shuddered. Metal creaked. Then, a steady bucking began.

Then, just as suddenly, he could feel a slowing in their movement, and a steady trembling, the familiar path of a decaying orbit. "We're going in."

"Then we're safe, mates. We're past the blockade!"

Weak cheering, punctuated by upchucking, and pungent smells filled the bay. Tears ran warmly down his face as he pulled himself back into the bunk. Memories flooded him. Real memories. Jack lay back and tried to think of other places and better times.

Amber stroked the white Flexalinks armor as she settled it into the large shipping trunk. Luckily, a woman of means such as the Duchess could afford massive baggage in her travels. The touch of her hands brought the faint flickering of Bogie's thoughts.

Where's the boss?

"I don't know, Bogie. But we're going to find out." The armor was cold, but the mind-link warm.

I—need him.

"Me, too, Bogie." Amber swallowed. It had been months since Jack's disappearance. Bogie's mind-link was incredibly weak. The parasitic life was no doubt losing its hold. But it was tough, unbelievably tough—it had survived seventeen years of cold sleep just as Jack had. Cold wasn't the way to kill Bogie. Maybe loneliness was. She lowered the lid and palm-locked the fasteners. And wherever he is, he needs us." She accessed the travel code. "First stop, the Triad's largest and most illegal cold sleep lab."

The hold doors opened. Jack listened to the clang and ring and prepared himself, pleasantly, for the inrush of new air—foreign, alien air, with its own spices and mixtures. The contractors were all on their feet, nudging forward, and he was caught in their wave, shoulder to shoulder, as they burst outside.

Inside—a long, gray tunnel, where the air was, if anything, more stale, more full of human misery, than the recycled stuff he'd been breathing for the last few days. Jack staggered to a halt, letting the press carry past him.

Stash stopped, too. He threw a look off his right shoulder and, with a grimy sleeve, wiped out a nearly opaque spot on the tunnel wall. "Look through here, mate," the man said.

Jack did. The starkness of nothingness hit him. He straightened, feeling for the first time the full impact of his situation. Lasertown was a dead moon mining community, her tunnels sprawled across the strip-mined landscape like an obscene spider's legs, the center domes its bloated body. Stash nudged him. "Nowhere to run 'ere, mate, unless you know where to run to." Then, whistling a merry tune, the New Aussie passed him by as he shouldered his duffel. Jack watched him go.

Alfredo came up behind him. He shook his head. "That's a bad un, Storm. You stay clear of him."

"Right." Jack shouldered his own duffel. Lying in the back of his mind like a dead thing was the realization that he'd been told all this before—he'd just never *realized* it. Walking out of here sooner or later was not going to be a possibility. Neither was working off his labor contract. He was going to be enslaved here for the rest of his life—however long or short it was destined to be.

They walked down the long length of corridor, the air more metallic and smothering every second, until it suddenly widened into a hall, where the air freshened somewhat, as an ancient recycler wheezed inside the arch. Massive bulkhead doors closed at their heels once every man was in.

He recognized Bull at the platform, transistorized speaker worn over his bulging adam's apple. Next to him was a woman, short-haired, nearly androgynous and supple as a gazelle. Jack had only a second to wonder who she was.

"Contractors, in a few moments, you will be given your crew berth assignments. You'll be joining crewmembers who have seniority here. Give them the respect that is their due—becoming a part of the team is something your lives as well as your cheeks depend on." The foreman's gaze swept them disdainfully. He deferred to the woman at his side. "Governor Franken."

"Contractors." Her voice, definitely feminine with overtones of a hidden strength, stilled the crowd immediately. How long, Jack wondered, had it been for some of them, hearing a woman's voice. He thought of Amber, too young for him, and yet he felt a pang. How could he ever have forgotten Amber?

"Contractors, it is customary at this time to allow those of you who feel you've been inducted unfairly to come forward. Your case will be reviewed. We're a mining community. Our lives depend on the happiness and reliability of our workers. Speak now," and she smiled, a smoky expression that faded before the echo of her words, "or forever hold your peace."

The crowd stirred. Jack found Stash elbowing

in next to him. The man looked at him. "Say a word and you're dead," he said.

"What?"

Stash nodded earnestly toward the governor. "Don't believe a word she says."

Behind him, two men argued in low, coarse voices. The querulous one said, "Me ex-wife did it, I tell you! She used an old plastiprint to authorize me contract."

"Hist and what if she did. Hold your tongue."

The governor pressed slender fingers to her throat mike. "No takers?"

Jack felt jostled as the second man gripped the first man in place. He shrugged. "What the hell." He stepped out and away from Stash. "I'd like my contract reviewed, your honor."

A hush settled over the rumbling crowd. Her eyes raked over Jack. "Well," she said, and smiled sadly. "An honest man." She looked to Bull, who stood mute. She waved to Jack. "You'll be escorted." She turned and left the platform, settling herself in a one-man cart.

Two immense men flanked Jack, and they walked to a four-man cart. Jack looked back. Stash's impervious smirk had vanished and his face had whitened. He gave a jaunty wave. "See ya, mate."

Not that he expected it to be a farewell, or even that his complaint be taken seriously. Jack only hoped he could survive what was going to happen to him, the price he would pay to see the hub of Lasertown, to get an overview of the deathtrap he planned to escape, an overview he would never have a chance to get cloistered in the stifling tunnels. The cart jerked forward, throwing him against the massive shoulders of the guard to his right, as they started toward the great, bloated belly of the spider city.

CHAPTER 7

"Lady—ah—"

"Styrene," Amber said, drawing herself up. Posture and bearing did more for this role than did makeup and dress. She looked at the solid man who positively seeped managerial qualities.

"Yes. Your, ah, baggage, far outweighs the allotment—"

She looked away, feigning unconcern, even as her heart did flip-flops. She did not want to leave Bogie behind! Suppose Jack needed him to fight his way out of this mess? "Yes, I'm aware. I have ... necessities. Charge the overweight to my account."

The Duchess' account. But, then, surely, the Duchess would have known this would occur once she'd decided to lend out her chip so boldly. And Amber would arrange to have it paid back.

"Madame Styrene, this is excessive even beyond overweight penalties."

Facing the other direction, Amber bit her lip. Damn! Why did Bogie have to weigh so much! Her other luggage carried a pittance of a ward-

97

robe. Even leaving the other two bags behind would barely make a dent. The ticket manager cleared his throat and continued, "I would advise shipping the trunk or storing it. . . ."

Amber watched the wave of passengers pass the centrifuge scales. The crowd was light, not many people spaced out this way. An idea seized her. She swung around to the manager. "I can't leave my trunk behind, citizen. Perhaps we can make other, er, arrangements."

His gaze swept her almost guiltily and he flushed, his large fleshy nose showing pink. "Lady Styrene, I hardly think this is the way to carry out a business—"

"Another ticket," Amber said haughtily. "Your passenger manifest appears to be a little light to me. I'll take my trunk on as another passenger. Cheaper than shipping it, eh? And certainly within your weight limits."

The manager licked his lips. "Well. Ah. A heavy passenger, but we've spaced heavier. Not human, of course, but . . . well. I don't see why not. Charge the fare to your account?"

Amber waved her hand. "You have my authorization. Now, I know you must be a dreadfully busy man. Is that all you needed me for?"

The manager shook her hand. "Thank you for the cooperation, Lady Styrene. Your boarding pass." He stamped the back of her hand lightly, lingeringly, before he released it.

Amber bolted up the ramps as she realized he must have had another kind of business arrangement in mind.

The ticket manager watched her go, more

graceful than a woman of her age and bearing might ordinarily be. Under her pancake make-up and heavily styled hair, she had a youthful beauty hidden that he, for a fleeting second, wished he might have had access to. But he had his orders. He returned to his office com and opened the lines.

Winton answered promptly.

"I had to let her on."

"Does she still have the baggage?"

"She bought a passenger ticket for the over-age. I could hardly refuse her, under the circumstances."

The man made a cold sound at the back of his throat. He tapped at the monitor's framework. "You could have, if I had ordered you to do so."

"Yes, well, if you had ordered." The ticket manager's mouth went dry. "I could, er, still do so. . . ."

"No. Never mind. Let her go."

"But I thought you didn't want her—"

Winton's dark eyes stared harshly at the man out of the visiphone screen. "You don't know what I want, other than for her to be delayed or refused, if possible, without raising suspicion. You have done what you can, within your limited scope. That *is* enough for you to know."

The com line went dead abruptly.

Winton sat back in his chair. He looked out the rosy pink wing of the Emperor's palace. The man should have been dead, and was not. Several times over, should have been dead. Perhaps this time, it would be wiser to stay in the background. Let the girl find him, if she could. If she could, he would deal with them both. If she could not, he was still as good as dead.

But not dead. No. And Winton wanted him dead. Dead as dead could be. He'd have to think of a way to handle it, after all.

But after Milos and Claron and even Malthen, Winton was beginning to think that this man led a charmed life. Impatiently, he tapped his fingers on the monitor framing.

Once aboard, Amber pulled off her wig and scrubbed her face of makeup, angrily, anxiously, as if she could change everything about herself. Rolf had taught her to read people. Now she knew she had the psychic ability that gave her the edge to do so and do so uncannily well—and she knew the ticket agent had let her aboard too easily. What had he been ordered to do? Delay her enough to miss the flight? Discourage her altogether without alerting her?

But she'd been made and she knew it. Jack had been ordered killed instead of chilled down and shipped out ... and if they followed her and she was lucky enough to find his trail—Jack was still a dead man. Damn Ballard. The Duchess' chip was as good as smoked. She'd have to throw the Duchess offboard, get her bags and get out without being noticed. Before they made port. Before, or it was no good at all.

Amber tapped on the viewscreens and watched latecomers boarding. She watched nervously, unseeing, thinking. The baggage slide was still quiet. Freight would go on last.

And that meant she needn't get on at all. Amber chewed on her lower lip. She spotted an elegant looking woman on the ramp, an older, equally elegant looking man at her elbow. Amber smiled. A little bit of pickpocketing in reverse ought to solve part of her problem—for the moment. A quick pat and the chip would change ownership. A tradesman's coveralls, and she'd have the trunk out of the freight loading area. She'd leave the other bags, not needing them now. Amber knew how to start over from scratch, she'd done it often enough, and this wasn't the only spaceport off Malthen. It didn't even dock the fastest ships. She suddenly decided she needed a very fast ship.

And once she picked up the trail out of the cold sleep lab, she'd think of something else.

CHAPTER 8

It didn't look like a torture chamber to him, but then, he hadn't been in a torture chamber before. Jack had few illusions about the appearance of the outer offices of the governor, though, for the two giants flanking him were tense as well as muscled. That made for a bad impression despite the unthreatening decor.

And the air smelled almost as bad in here as it did out there.

"Sit," the big man on his left said.

Jack sat. He looked out the large windowed wall of the outer office and saw the sprawling mining community below. Drab. Gray. Sterile. The two men started to leave. Jack looked up. "No company?"

They grinned. "You aren't going anywhere."

As the door shut behind them, Jack saw they were right. The interior walls of this place were heavily fortified. He stood up and walked to the window behind the computer bank. The dome overhead shut off most of the view of space. He saw no sign of the planet the moon encircled.

Once down in the tunnels, he wasn't likely to get a view of it ever.

He rubbed his arms. He turned and looked at the armored door. In the suit, he could have walked through it. He savored his newly gained memories. Everything was in its place, that he could expect, with the exception of Stash. He remained enigmatic.

There was a snick, a slight movement in the air pressure. Jack swiveled and saw that the door to the inner offices had just barely opened. Sound bled out. He heard the governor's voice.

"What's the damage look like?"

"Tunnel 102 is shut down. You can override the computer if you want. I'm told the crew got an insulator panel up in time. They're asking for official action." A crisp male voice, blurred slightly by the com lines. Jack relaxed a little and stepped closer to listen.

"I can't do that. The tunnels are not part of the main installation. If Lasertown is the spider, the mining tunnels are the webs. It'll be damn difficult proving the Thraks strafed it on purpose and that it wasn't hit by debris from the embargo lines. Override the recycling computer if you think the leak is plugged. And get the crew back in there to make repairs. Dock them two pay periods if anyone refuses to go."

"But governor—they want protection."

The woman swore softly. Then she said, "They're drilling below the surface. That's all the protection they get."

"That's not enough when the Thraks come in."

"It's all they're going to get! I have to protect the main domes. The scramble and the armament stay focused in on the main domes."

Jack stood quietly and listened to the angry buzz of a disconnected com line. He stretched his neck thoughtfully. Almost before he had a chance to draw a breath, an incoming call chimed.

"Governor Franken?"

The woman sighed imperceptibly and answered, "Yes, Reverend Wesley. How may I help you?"

"There is some concern in the hotel because of the latest raid."

"Everything is fine, reverend."

"There are rumors of a disaster in the mines."

She answered without even a pause. Jack grimaced. The woman could definitely think on her feet. "Rumor, only. One of the recycling computers has a malfunction. It showed a blowout and shut down one of the newer tunnels. But there's no leak and we have it under control."

"Ah." The softly modulated male voice paused. "Perhaps then we can discuss our petition?"

"This is really not the time, Reverend Wesley." Governor Franken did not strain to keep the irritation from her voice.

Her caller pressed. "We've been delayed several months already, governor. I've had an opportunity to review some of the on-surface strip mining projects—"

"How did you get hold of that! That information is confidential." Now Franken was no longer bored and angry, but just angry.

"Let's just say that we Walkers have believers everywhere. It was given to us by someone who believes that we have a genuine archaeological find that we must investigate, not mine. Your plans for the area will destroy the evidence this moon's unique conditions preserve."

"Oh, come on now," Franken snapped. "If you think Jesus Christ walked on this . . . this rock, you're more than fanatics, you're insane. Look at it out there beyond the domes, reverend!"

"The ways of the Lord are mysterious. Who can say if this moon was always lifeless? And if it has been, who can say how the Lord chose to visit it, if visit it He did. You haven't answered our petition."

Jack felt the tension fairly boiling out of the inner office. He stood very still, half-holding his breath.

"And I don't intend to, yet, reverend, until I've had time to review it properly. The site of contention is on the dark side and I have yet to see any visual evidence to corroborate your assertion that there is a find. I like to have some evidence myself before making decisions."

Jack thought that it would be damned difficult getting an aerial photographic assessment, what with the Thraks picking away at Lasertown.

The male voice said firmly, "At least that's better than a denial. And when do you think you'll be able to make time?"

Franken's nails clicked impatiently on the desk top. "If you can get these Thraks off our backs, it might help."

A dry chuckle. "That would be miraculous

work. I'm sorry, governor, but that is not in my province. However," a pause, "to give you some incentive, I've been informed that my superior is en route. *He* knows how to apply pressure. Good day, governor."

The line buzzed open and the speaker cut off abruptly, leaving dead silence. He heard the woman murmur, "You're not so bad at it, yourself."

Jack walked back to the couch where he'd been deposited. Walker evidence here? He rubbed his chin thoughtfully. That would be something to see.

The door opened and Governor Franken emerged. She smiled, a whitened, strained gesture. "Well," she said. "Not many contractors take me up on my offer."

"I'm sure it was not a wise decision on my part."

The woman leaned against the computer console. She showed a sleek amount of leg, having changed her protective gear for in-office wear. She tilted her head to one side. "You're as intelligent as you look."

Jack answered with a small nod of his own. He stood up. "I'm a free mercenary, Governor Franken, not a contractor. But I'm not stupid enough to think that the labor contract you hold on me has any loopholes. If it had—I wouldn't have made it this far."

She smiled, a loveless expression that etched vertical lines to either side of her mouth. "You may not make it much farther if you decide to threaten me at this point."

"Not threaten. But free mercenaries share a certain camaraderie, if you will."

"As well as reputations." Governor Franken reached behind her and picked up a smokestick from the computer console. She lit it, and an incense-scented gray-blue smoke drifted out as she drew on it deeply, then exhaled. "Done anything that we might have heard about, even way out here on the frontier?"

"I was in the assault group that took out General Gilgenbush's satellite."

Her eyebrows went up. "You surprise me again ... whatever your name is."

"Last I heard, it was still Jack. Jack Storm."

"And what kind of labor were you shanghaied for?"

"Demolitions. I got myself demoted to welding, however."

She drew again, tension lines easing out of her face and bared neckline almost perceptibly. "I would think a man with your background would find demolitions a natural."

"I find staying alive even more natural," Jack answered dryly.

"So I don't get to hear about your injustices? Stories about your enemies?"

"If I told you stories about my enemies, you might find yourself working down in the tunnels next to me."

"Really?" Franken straightened abruptly. "So if you don't want your contract contested, what do you want?"

Jack smiled. He walked over to the window and looked out. He had a nearly 200 degree overview of Lasertown. "I just wanted to see the lay of the land, governor." His smile stayed as he turned back to her. Thrakian raids could camouflage an escape very nicely.

"Just the land?" Franken asked gently. "It doesn't pay to question the contract. If you managed to break it, you would still be in hock to the company. For transportation, food, gear, and so forth. Talk, in Lasertown, isn't cheap."

"I guessed that."

The silence that fell in the office tingled along his spine. He was caught in the spider's web and the spider's lair. And he had the distinct feeling that this spider lady could be most poisonous. He might gain freedom of a certain kind if he stayed here—but he would also be watched more closely. He remained smiling. "Thank you for the tour."

His smile was not reflected in her cold eyes as they stood, face to face. Governor Franken hesitated. "Stay with me."

Surprise warmed him. Before he could answer, she added, "I don't normally have to ask. Or care to. Maybe it's your eyes."

Jack sensed an escape he hadn't hoped for. "Would it do me any good?"

"No." She shook her head sadly. Her sleek dark brown hair cupped about her face. "I'm trapped here as much as you are, and only meeting the quota will set me free. And I can't meet the quota with an inadequate labor force."

"Then let me see the contract. I want to know who set me up."

She shook her head again, halfheartedly. "You won't see it in there."

Jack stepped to the console and monitor. He looked back at her over his shoulder. "Access it for me."

With a soft sigh, the governor leaned over and did so, her fingers flying over the keys with an ease that suddenly reminded Jack, achingly, of Amber. It was a memory he didn't need in his way right now, but she stayed there anyway, clinging determinedly to the edge of his thoughts as the screen filled with the blowup of his contract. He scanned. He knew nothing of the names, labor broker or even the lab that had chilled him down. A brief history was nearly all fabrication except for one item.

He'd been listed as a veteran.

Winton. Only Winton would know he was a veteran. It wasn't listed in his records when he'd been assigned to ranger on Claron. No one was to know of his background when they gave him a new life. It had been easy enough to lose in the electronic transfer of his real history.

Jack terminated the picture. He stood and found himself very close to the woman. But the temptation had been considerably disturbed by Amber and he found himself changing his plans.

Franken smiled poignantly. "Last chance. Let me give you some pleasure before I have to give you some pain. I can't send you back without it. Otherwise, the contractors will think I'm going soft. I can't let them think they can challenge me or their contracts."

He shrugged. "Another time. Anyway," and

he reviewed the landscape of Lasertown, memo-
rizing its weak spots, and then sweeping her
with a different kind of look, "the view was
worth it."

She flushed angrily. She pressed a button on
the computer console. "You'll find that you'll be
paying a very high price for this visit, Mr. Storm.
Next time, it will be considerably cheaper and
much less nerve-racking to buy a map." She
ground out her smokestick viciously as the door
opened. She didn't look up at her two assis-
tants. "Give Mr. Storm a sample of the tangler
for wasting my time," she ordered.

Their big hands closed around his arms. Jack
shrugged. "There's no such thing as a free lunch,"
he said, as they lifted him off his feet and removed him from the office.

CHAPTER 9

Amber clung to the cold prefab sheeting that passed for a wall. She pressed her thin body to it and wished with every nerve she had that she could become invisible. The wall sheeting cooled her . . . perhaps she'd even pass an infrared scan. She could only pray.

Tiny beads of sweat rolled up on her brow and for the first time she knew what was meant by a cold sweat. She felt it trickle down over her eyes where the beads clung like iridescent zirconias on her false eyelashes. She sensed, more than heard, the electronic sweep. Dear god, let it pass her by. She'd found all she needed to get to Jack, now, please, let the sensors pass her over.

No klaxons started. Amber felt confident enough to take a short breath. If she were traveling alone, unburdened, she just might get out of this alive. But she had to go back for Bogie. She might be trailed there and, then again, she might not.

She didn't want to die way out here, suns and

moons away from Malthen, and equally far away from Jack. She'd been weeks scraping by, looking, listening, spying, accessing forbidden systems and finally found his trail among a shipment of cold storage labor contractors, most of whom had been inducted for near lifetime servitude. As she clung to the prefab corridor and tried to still the wild-bird beating of her heart, she knew that if she were found, she'd be killed.

Just for knowing what she'd found out.

The original chiller and shipper had been killed.

Amber willed herself to wait through another sweep. The minute electronic probes set off her psychic senses like insane alarms, pinging and ponging before they passed on. She took a deep breath. Now was the time to run for it.

Amber fled.

Jack struggled to wake. A net of fire seared every nerve in his body and as he lifted his head, he felt as though his neck were broken and once having lifted his head, it would bob forever at the broken end of his body. His skin crawled and he lifted a hand to stare at it. When his eyes finally focused, he stared in disbelief, expecting to see blistered and welted skin.

He forced his head to stop shaking. He wiggled a few fingers experimentally. Slowly, as if they'd been asleep and then awakened with excruciating pins and needles, a wave of pain began at his fingertips, then receded. Jack was vaguely grateful he'd only nine fingers to assault him instead of ten.

His hand dropped limply back onto the bunk. He heard a man groaning. Then, the way a drowning man recognizes his own gulping, he realized he was the one sobbing.

The pain left his right hand. Jack turned his head to look at his hand. Other than a rosy blush to his skin, there was no sign of the torment. His head throbbed. He screwed his eyes shut and tried to remember. He'd been taken out of the office and then to a lab. A chair with restraints. And then a net of webbing was draped over him. Jack felt intensely sick to his stomach and decided he'd remembered enough.

Governor Franken obviously did not believe in token pain.

A cocky voice intruded on his memories. "What's this, mate? Awake enough to groan? And they told us you wouldn't come round till sometime tomorrow. Hey. I bet you'd like a cup of that cold water. Soothes the nerve fire from the tangler, they tell me."

Jack twisted his head in the other direction. Stash squatted on the floor next to his bunk, grinning.

"You are awake, then. Well, what'd you say? What'll you give me for a cup of water?"

His mouth and tongue felt like insulating foam. He worked to get his jaws moving and managed a weak, "Stuff it."

Insolence beamed back at him. "Look at that!" Stash dipped out a cup and offered it to Jack anyway. Half of it slipped out thanks to muscles that remained slack no matter how hard he tried to drink, but what he got down cooled the raging fire inside.

Stash relaxed back into his squat, hands dangling from over his knees. "You know, mate, they say pain's instructive. Sure taught us a lot. Ain't none of us willing to fool around with her ladyship, contract or not. No, we'll beg, borrow or steal our way free, but screw the system. Look what the tangler did to you, and you an innocent man."

Jack blinked. "Am I?" he croaked.

"Course you are. Anyone here can see that. Innocent as a newborn baby."

Jack closed his eyes wearily. If newborn babies could, and had, waded through fields of blood and broken bodies. But then, he was a soldier, a weapon. The thought echoed strangely in his mind.

Stash pulled up the thermal blanket and tucked it under his still wet chin. "They docked you three days' pay, mate. You might as well go back to sleep an' enjoy it. Don't worry. We'll get you up and suited in time." Stash lowered his voice. "We welders are gettin' premium time, what with the Thraks blowin' away the bulkheads and such on the tunnels. Worth our weight in gold, we are." And Stash gave a nasty chuckle.

Thraks, Jack thought, drifting back into a kind of sleep, half on fire and half merely bone weary unto death. God, he hated Thraks.

Amber?

She woke, quickly, as the tough-edged voice knifed into her consciousness. "Yeah, Bogie?"

Find Jack?

She allowed herself a tired smile. "Almost. When we get to Wheeling Way Station, we need to transfer. It may take us a while ... Wheeling's tough, but we'll make it." She was curled up on top of the immense traveling trunk that held the Flexalink suit. She'd been asleep with the corner pressing into her cheek. The freight bay was cold and Amber shivered.

But ... find Jack?

She scrubbed the back of her hand over her eyes. What made her think Bogie would understand even half of what she said? "Bogie, I found out where he went. And I'm taking you there."

Good. A pause, then, *Any trouble, Bogie fight for you.*

Amber laughed soundlessly. She had no doubt he would, if she could manage to suit up. But she knew how Jack wrestled for control endlessly over the berserker spirit that occupied the battle armor. She wouldn't have a chance. Bogie'd have the way station blown into deep-space debris before she'd learned how to stop him. "Thanks, pal," she said. "I hope that won't be necessary."

Fighting is good, Bogie protested.

"Only to survive," Amber soothed him. "Now shut up. I'm trying to sleep."

Oh. Silence. Then, *What is sleep?*

"Bogie!"

Right.

Amber closed her eyes. The freight bay lost its chill only when she slept. When she woke, she'd have to figure out how to steal some food and

117

use the toilet again. Not that they'd do much to her if they found out she was stowing away. No, not much—just jettison her in deepspace with the rest of the garbage. She sighed. She'd gotten this far. She wondered how Jack was doing.

Stash gave a blissful sigh. "Shift premiums. Like gold, they are. We'll be out of here in no time." He slapped Jack on the back. "And you wear that suit like a glove, mate."

Jack grunted in answer.

His companion sounded affronted. "I show you a golden opportunity and I get ignored."

"C'mon, Stash. You make more money from smuggling than you do from welding."

"That may be as may be . . . but if it buys the ticket, what's the difference? We're outta here."

Jack looked down the long line of tunnels. He'd never get used to them. They blasted out rock and welded the interconnections together like worn casings, segments unfolded in a ceaseless line. Weld and seal, quickly, so the crews behind them could come in and sift through the newly blasted rock. If they were lucky, the demolition crew would find a new vein and work would slow for a while. If they weren't, the tunnels would have to stretch far out of the way—and if they were absolutely cursed, the Thraks would hit them. And there was always work for the welders.

The shift car had let them off at their intersection, not far from the barracks. Jack stretched his gaze, trying to rest his eyes from all the close work he'd done during the shift. Muscles bunched across his back as he moved his tired arms. He was dropping weight and muscle, try as he would to stay fit.

"Well, mate, will you look at that?"

Jack slowed. There, up against the gray tunnel wall, in a pile of Lasertown rock and ash, a tiny, feathery gray-green plant grew. He bent over it. Even in the sterility of Lasertown, something was still trying to grow. Disinfecters sprayed the inner tunnels twice a day to discourage mold and fungi from growing ... but this was a seed, brought in perhaps on the boot of another worker from some other job site planets away, and it had found a way to survive.

Stash touched the fronds gently with his glove. Jack tensed. "Leave it, Stash."

"Course, I will, mate. Whattya know." He straightened and walked off whistling, his intercom staticky with the noise even though he had his helmet popped.

Jack looked after him. He had little doubt that Stash had recognized the plant and had plans for coming back later, in case it could be cured and used to his advantage. He sighed and set off after his welding partner.

Tension was thick at the cafeteria. Stash's air of happiness rankled the other, tired crews. He raised an eyebrow and looked across at Jack. "What're you going to do on your day off, Jack, my boy?"

Jack gave him a look and then answered, slowly, "I hadn't thought about it. Go into the domes, I guess."

"Ah. And what about you, Fritzi?"

The grizzled, big shouldered man in front of Stash, his back bowed as though it were a shield to keep out the New Aussie, grumbled something low.

Stash says, "What's that? I didn't hear you."

The big man turned around. "I said," he rumbled, "that some people didn't get a day off, thanks to you."

Stash's eyes got big and round. "Thanks to me," he repeated, as he set his tray down on the auto line and watched it start to fill. "Thanks to me? Is that gratitude, I ask you? Did I give you those vices, Fritzi? No. I simply work my fingers to the bone to keep you satisfied with them. So if you have to put some double time or triple time on my timecards to pay off your debts, don't blame me, Fritzi."

Alfredo Boggs picked up his tray from the front of the line. He glowered down at Stash. "Leave him alone, Stash."

Stash lifted his hands in the air and affected an injured look. "Didn't lay a glove on him."

Fritzi growled and turned back in line.

Jack shrugged off the tension. He looked about and saw Perez. "What's up?"

"It's th' sleeping sickness. Got another man off second shift."

"What are you talking about?"

The olive-skinned man looked at him. "Where you have been? So far out in the tunnels you don't know what's going on? Did you ever wonder why we're all crewed together? Because they don't want us mingling with the old crew, that's why."

Stash scratched the back of his neck. "They're all looney, from what I hear."

The cable layer shrugged. "Maybe so. All I know is, they do loco things."

Jack hadn't heard much but whispers in the barracks. The hair rose on the back of his neck and he tried to ignore it. "What kind of things?"

"They walk off."

"Walk off?"

"Without suits or nothin', man. They just walk off. And they don't get far, you know what I mean. But they don't care. I heard the other night one of Bull Quade's men tried to stop one—and he damn near killed the Sweeper trying to get outside the tunnels." Perez' voice dropped to a near reverent hush.

"Bad drugs."

Perez bristled at Stash. "Yeah, man. What I hear is, if it's bad drugs, they got 'em from you. But no, that can't be it. It's been going on since Lasertown opened up. But the ore is so rich, they can't leave it alone. Not to mention the rubies."

"What is it? Some kind of narcosis from the air maybe?"

"They're loco, that's what it is."

"Well, I'm hungry." Stash reached out, bodily lifted the smaller man from their path and moved him aside. Then Stash headed for the food dispensers.

Perez made a face at Jack. "You be careful, man," he said.

"Yeah. I'll do that. You, too."

The cable layer nodded and sauntered off. Jack

went in search of a food tray. He'd wondered why they hadn't been melded with the old crew. If there was a problem, it explained why. The contractors filling the cafeteria were a glum, intense lot this mid-shift.

Stash grinned at Jack and said, in a very loud whisper, "I figure, what with all the triple time that's being done on my card and with all the money I'm making from my little side enterprises, I'll be able to buy out in, oh, say—year and a half at the most."

Jack felt a quiver go up his spine. Most of the men here were in for two to five years. A lifetime in Lasertown, with little to look forward to but a walk to the other side of the town or maybe an afternoon in the hydroponics gardens. The fact that they'd earned this future, in one way or another, didn't make it any easier to live. "Lay off, Stash," he said.

"Righto, mate. Course, lookit you. Maybe you got something going with the spider lady, right? No need to work out your contract. Maybe you could introduce Fritzi here. From what I hear, he likes that kind of thing. The tangler would just make him tingle."

The volcano of a man in front of him exploded, smashing the food tray into Stash's face, then grabbing him and making a fairly good attempt at mopping the floor with him.

Two other crewmen took the opportunity to jump Jack. He shook off one and found himself toe to toe with the other. Adrenalin surged. By god, it felt good to be in a fight, Jack thought, and swung.

Food slung through the air like the garbage it was, great lumpy, soggy gobs of soy protein. Jack ducked. The miner slugging it out with him took a deep, happy breath.

"This is great," he said.

Jack agreed and swung again, connecting with a jolt he felt all the way to his elbow. The miner dropped, still grinning ear to ear.

Stash appeared on the backswing. "C'mon, mate, let's get out of here."

The entire cafeteria had erupted with brawling bodies. Jack felt more alive than he had in weeks. The melee invigorated him.

"Why?"

"Th' Sweepers! I don't want to lose all my hard earned credits. Follow me."

Jack almost made it to the cafeteria doors.

He didn't feel invigorated when he left the foreman's office and even Stash looked a little pale.

He caught up with Jack. "Hey, mate, how was I to know?"

"To know what? I don't mind being fined for the fight—I enjoyed that. No, it was being hooked with your pimping and narcotics dealing that bothers me." Jack felt the rage burning through him, but it wasn't clean anger this time. It was anger that would have to fester because he couldn't do anything about it.

Stash shrugged. "You knew I was hustling."

"And you know I'm nothing more to you than a work partner. Why didn't you stand up for me in there?"

"And do you think they would have listened? Come on, Jack. This is war, us against the rest of them."

"No, that's just it, Stash. We're all in this together. You don't seem to get that, do you? Lasertown is a cruddy, miserable excuse for life . . . but we're all in this together. That's the only way we're getting out of here."

Stash rubbed his bruised face where Fritzi had smashed a food tray into it. He shook his head. "You're still a baby, Jack." He shouldered past him in the hallway. "I guess that's one o' the things I like about you." He snickered. "You're like a breath of fresh air."

Infuriated, Jack watched him leave, then followed after. Hall security cameras watched his every move. He looked up at them briefly. In his frustration with Stash, he had uttered a very potent truth. If all the miners broke out together, there was nothing on this rock that could hold them.

Amber didn't think she could get much colder and live. She paused, huffing and puffing, in the shadowy corner of a side street. Her breath no longer frosted on the air, her insides now just as cold as her outsides. She hauled the trunk alongside her, its bottom scraping the sleet covered streets. She had none of the things she needed to survive here at Wheeling—no money, no E.P. suit, not even a jacket. There would always be hope tomorrow, in the daylight, if this godforsaken planet *had* a daylight.

She tucked her hands in her armpits.

Actually, the planet was far from godforsaken. It was a Walker outpost built as a jumpoff point for further exploration. Just before dusk, the streets had been full of them, snug in their robes, even the women. Amber took her hands out and breathed on them hopefully. If she could just keep her fingers limber until someone came out of a bar or gambling pit . . . then she could lift some plastic and charge for a night's rest.

She stood on one numbed leg and then the other. Nights were always worse, always, when things were bad. She wouldn't give up till morning. There was always another day. Always, she told herself.

Unless she froze to death on the street tonight.

She thought momentarily of pawning Bogie. He was a pain to drag around anyway, but she didn't have enough coin for a locker at the port. But she doubted anyone here would value the armor. And it would be a lot tougher to steal back than a ring or charge card.

Amber discarded the idea.

She flexed her fingers. So close and yet so far.

A white, frosty cloud of warm air puffed onto the end of the street not far from where Amber huddled. She watched it with a new sense of hope.

"I suggest we retire for the evening, sir. You've an early morning ahead of you."

More than one man came out on the street. Amber disliked the odds, but then decided she could create enough chaos on the sleet-and-icy streetway to offset that.

An older man—she couldn't see him well in the halo of light from the street lamps—rubbed his gloved hands together. "I don't see Wheeling near as often as I should. I like to keep an eye on what we built."

The younger man gave a polite laugh. "It's no longer ours, sir."

"No, indeed. The leading edge of the frontier, with all its roughness, seems to have claimed it. Some good work for you, eh, if I decide to go on alone?"

"Sir! You can't . . . the dig . . ."

"Ah. You want to see the dig site."

The younger man straightened to an awkward, beanpole height. "More than anything!"

"It's not been authorized."

"No, sir."

Amber gave her fingers one last rub. She'd have to leave the trunk in the alley and come back in a few hours. But the snow was drifting over it already, and she doubted anyone would find it. She prepared for the bump and hit, and dash across the road.

It was now or never.

Amber threw herself out of the alley. She bumped the older man, found his plastic immediately, tripped him down and sent him rolling into the second man. Then she ran for it.

But the second man jumped the body of the first agilely. Amber heard him grunt, his warm breath grazed her shoulder, and then she was hit herself, tumbling through the air. She hit the ground and skidded, her breath sobbing from her lungs, the plastic card cutting into her frozen fingers. She lay gasping for breath as the young man kicked her over onto her back.

His angry brown eyes blazed down at her, his face blurred by the street light. "Even in Wheeling, slag, you have to have guts to attack a saint."

Amber caught the ragged edges of her breath. It was cold and iced through her bruised chest. "Saint or not, I got to live."

The older man ambled over and put a hand on his friend's arm as he looked down mildly. "What have you caught, Lenska?"

"A thief." The young man kicked her wrist to knock the card out of her hand. The blow on her iced bone was even more shocking than it might have been and Amber gasped.

"That's enough, Lenska." The older man bent over. "She looks harmless enough to me."

"She? That's female?"

"I think so. Yes," and the man laughed softly. "When it wants to be. What are you doing out here?"

"Surviving." Amber stood up stiffly.

"Not well. And thieving is no way to do it." The older man looked at the beanpole. "Here's your first challenge. How would you reform her?"

Amber felt sullen as the young man looked over. He grimaced. "I wouldn't even try."

The old man tsked. He looked at her. "Then you try to reform yourself. Name your punishment."

She thought of the warm robes she'd seen the others wearing. "Make me a nun," she said, only a little sarcastically. The one called Lenska kicked hard.

"Really? Repent and become a nun? Would you?"

"I'd do anything to get warm again," Amber answered honestly, and a little hopefully, for the older man had a wealth of humor in his eyes.

"Sir!" gasped the beanpole. "That's sacrilege."

"No," laughed the elder. "That's realism. Come with me, then, and I'll see what I can do. But only until you get warm. I won't have the robes of a Walker disgraced."

"But, sir, you can't take on a—a street thief."

"And why not?"

"You're spacing out tomorrow morning."

The brisk walking brought some feeling back to Amber's legs and feet. She began to shiver violently. The old man noticed and removed an outer cloak. He draped it over her shoulders. "Ah, yes. That's right. That is a problem. Unless, of course, you'd like to come with us."

Amber shook her head, her teeth chattering, but she forced out, "No ... no, sir. I've got places to go."

"So have I. But I can't leave you here to the weather and the streets. That's a Walker failing. Once having found work that needs to be done, we don't like to walk away from it. And I think you need some re-working, young lady, unless I miss my guess."

Amber stopped short and dropped the warm cloak in the snow. "No," she said. "I'm not anybody's project. I have to find somebody. Thanks, anyway."

And Lenska blurted, "You can't take her to Lasertown, Colin."

Amber blinked. "Lasertown?" she repeated numbly. She bent quickly and picked up the cloak. "On the other hand," she said, "I did say I'd even become a nun to get warm."

St. Colin smiled broadly. "There've been worse reasons," he answered and took her chilled hand in his.

CHAPTER 10

"Well," St. Colin said, as they settled aboard the compartment suite. He had said little during the night or in the morning when Amber rescued the snow-laden trunk from the alleyway, though his magnificent eyebrows had danced a little with surprise. He waited until Lenska left, though the shambling youth had not wanted to, and had glared at Amber when he finally did.

Amber, meanwhile, snuggled into her new clothes which were courtesy of the Walker church. Her fingers fairly glowed with rosy warmth. She sat down and drew her legs up inside the robe, and wrapped her arms about her knees. "Yes?"

Colin sat as well. "You don't expect me to believe you wish to become a nun or even a convert. What is there at Lasertown you expect to find?"

"I'm not all that interested in Lasertown," Amber returned. "Any place is better than this iceberg."

He shook his head, wearily. "No, my street thief. I expect the truth from you. You're not from Wheeling, either, or you'd have been dressed for the cold. Therefore, you're in transit. And you know what to expect from Lasertown, I think. It's a dead moon mining community. By going there with me, you are, as the ancient saying has it, going from the frying pan into the fire as ill-prepared as you are. Treat me with respect and intelligence, child. What do you want in Lasertown?"

Amber's nose twitched. She tossed her head and looked at him warily. "All right. I have a friend I think was sent there."

"Sent?"

"Illegal labor contract. I think he was put into cold sleep and shipped out under one."

The religious man sat quietly, thoughts shadowing mild brown eyes and the air conditioning in the cabin ruffling the thin fringe of hair he had left. Labor contracts were the closest thing to slave labor. Difficult to stop from being made and still more difficult to breach. He'd been handsome, once, she thought, even as she looked away from his gaze which she found hard to bear. Finally, he cleared his throat. "Perhaps, child, you were merely abandoned again."

"No! He had no reason to sign up. I know he was taken forcibly by someone who wants him out of the way."

"Who would want to do such a thing?"

She rolled her eyes. "Believe me, St. Colin, you don't want to know. But there are reasons, all right. Anyway, if I can just get to him, I can prove who he is and they'll have to let him go."

"Break contract?"

"That's right. I've been tracking him for a couple of months."

"I see." The Walker fingered his crude cross as though it helped him to meditate. "Just who is this man?"

Amber hesitated for just a moment, then shrugged. "He's Jack Storm, and he's a member of the Emperor's new Guard. Whoever messed with him is going to be real sorry."

St. Colin's eyebrows danced again and his face paled slightly. "Storm, you said? Kind of sandy haired, tired blue eyes? Plain face, but striking?"

"That's him! You know him?"

The man sank back in his chair and mumbled. "Indeed, I do." He thumbed on the intercom. "All right, Lennie. Tell the pilot he has my okay to take off."

Amber's head swiveled. "What?"

Colin shrugged. "You didn't think I'd take you along for the ride, my dear, without knowing why you wanted to go? This old hide has been a target once or twice in its lifetime, too. As a matter of fact, this Jack of yours is responsible for saving it the last time out."

Amber shoved her legs out of her curled up position and stood up. "You mean you were going to kick me off?"

"Of course, if you hadn't told the truth or I didn't like what I heard. I would have let you keep the robes, though. I do have some Christian charity." He beckoned at her. "I suggest you sit down now. The take off will be more than a little bumpy."

Amber sat as the ship began to thrum. She swallowed heavily, disliking the thrust of a ship taking off from full gravity.

St. Colin fished around in his robe pocket, peeled off something and handed her a tiny patch. "Put that behind your ear. It's Tri-scopalomine. Does wonders for take offs."

She did as she was told.

The Walker settled back. His dark blue robes shimmered over the plain taupe jumpsuit beneath it. "How would anyone get their hands on Jack? He's damn near invincible wearing that armor of his."

"He wasn't wearing it. It's in the trunk I'm lugging along."

"I see." Colin half-closed his eyes in thought. "Do you think it's wise bringing something like that along to Lasertown?"

She grinned. "I figure Jack might need all the persuasion he can find."

"Yes, well, you're probably right there." He smiled back. "And having me on your side won't hurt any, either."

Their conversation was interrupted as the ship began its spiral launch, the force of its thrust pushing them deep into the heavily padded chairs. But Amber closed her eyes in appreciation of St. Colin's intuitive grasp of the situation. All hell was going to break loose once she got the suit to Jack!

*   *   *

Jack wouldn't look at Stash on the march back down to the tunnels. Stash's scarred eyebrow winged upward.

"You look a bit peeved, mate."

"Not only did you wipe out your credit line, but mine, too. Guilt by association," Jack pointed out.

"Well, there's that, but look. There's money to be made here and I don't mean by grubbing down in those tubes. There's dreams and privileges to be bought and sold."

"I don't deal in those."

"Neither do I, mate, normally. Look, stick wi' me and we'll be fine. Promise. You'll have your contract bought out in a year's time."

Finding Stash's hand on his wrist in a pretense of earnestness, Jack stopped. "I don't need to stick with you, *mate*, but I have noticed that you seem to stick by me. Now why is that?"

Stash drew himself back. He brushed his thick black hair out of his face. "Well, now. That'd be hard to say, exactly. Maybe it's because we're both the same kind of man."

Jack snorted as he turned away and began striding back to the barracks. He had enough time to suit up and get out on shift without being docked.

"Now look," Stash called, as he hurried to catch up. "See here. We're not miners or welders, like that lot. I'm a bit out of fortune right now, but I don't intend to stay that way."

"Not like me." Jack shook his head. "You're nothing like me, Stash."

"Maybe I'm more like you than you think,"

the man returned quietly. Then his bravado over-rode him. "We'll both be back on top, you see, and by this weekend, we'll have a couple of girls waiting for us in the domes, and you'll be happy with old Stash for providin' all the comforts of home."

Jack lengthened his stride until the other fell puffing by the wayside. But something Stash had said rankled at him. The drill instructor for the Emperor had repeatedly said, "No suit, no soldier." But even Stash knew better, instinc-tively reaching beyond the trappings to the basic core of a man. He was a soldier. He hadn't had much opportunity to fight lately, but he had an enemy and he was damned if he was going to retreat now.

He suited up. One of the small transport cars was still on track. He checked its programing. Evidently the shift had gone on ahead and had not needed this extra car. He started it up. Stash shouted, made a lumbering jump and caught it, pulling himself into the last seat. Jack left his com off, not wanting to hear any more pseudo-carefree Aussie chat. Fellow soldier or not, Stash was, in almost any way he could name, thor-oughly despicable.

He tapped in his ID number at the work sta-tion computer. It flashed a "Fifteen minute pen-alty for lateness" at him and settled back to opaque. Jack shrugged. It could have been worse. He stepped over the cables being laid by the cable crew, squinted at the temporary arc lights and went on down the line.

The small, crumpled deepsuit that was Alfredo Boggs waved to him as he walked onto the job site. Jack flipped on his com lines and went over.

"Sorry to see you go with him," Boggs said. "That was a bum rap."

Jack laughed. "Life can be a bum rap. Maybe I deserved it."

"Maybe."

"What's being hooked up?"

"A T-joint here, as soon as demo is finished. We've got seismo readings that say we should reach a gem deposit in that direction, but the foreman wants to keep options open."

"Right. Where do you want me?"

"Right here next to me. This is a tricky seam— keeps wanting to bulge on me, and you do nice work."

Jack nodded. It was a dubious honor. The tunnel was already being pressurized. If the seam blew while either of them were working on it, they might not live to realize what had happened. On the other hand, Boggs was acknowledging he had a deft hand with the welder. He grabbed an iron and lit it up. He paid no attention as Stash trailed in and went to work in another direction.

"Poor pay for a good day's work." Boggs heaved a sigh as he wrenched his helmet off and set it back on a hook. The suit technician stood by, waiting impatiently, as he unsuited.

Jack helped him shrug out of the heavy garment. "It's a living some of us have to settle for," he said.

Boggs wagged a bony finger at the tech. "See I get a full charge next time! I'm not usin' the damn thing to walk off this rock in. I don't want to run out of nothin' if I'm workin' a double shift. Comprende?"

The tech grimaced and threw the suit on a rack. Boggs shook his head. "Nobody cares about nothin' down here."

"Except you."

He straightened and gave Jack a hard look. "I'm shift manager. I got to care. Besides . . . you kids don't call me Pops for nothing. I've twice outlived most of you."

Jack kept his expression under control. What would Pops think if he knew Jack was twice as old as he looked, thanks to cold sleep? Probably not much. He doubted if much got by Pops. He peeled off his own suit. Pops might not intend to walk off, but Jack did. He'd noticed that the air supply was kept low and had wondered how he could circumvent that. Pops had just given him a clue.

He followed the wiry middle-aged man to the showers and the lockers beyond. Water here was more than scarce. He got fifteen seconds of heavy steam to open his pores, a rag to soap with and another rag to wash off with. He'd taken longer showers on his battle cruiser over Milos. But he did feel cleaner. Jack grabbed down a disposable towel and padded toward the lockers.

He heard Stash's voice before he rounded the corner. Jack grimaced. Last on the line and first off, that was Stash. He was giving that sly smile of his, baiting the mountain man Fritzi.

"Hey, mate, y' know what's coming up? The weekend, I'll tell you, that's what. And you know where I'm going to head? The Velvet Pit, eh?"

Fritzi rumbled. He stood, shirt off, in front of his plastic locker, jaws working.

"Uh-oh," Boggs said, as he came in behind Jack. Others crowded the locker row, too.

The big man thundered, "You don't get a weekend. They took you in for punishment for starting the fight."

"Oh, no, y'got it all wrong. I lost me credits, not my privileges. No, I still got my weekend and I plan to enjoy it." Stash gave an exaggerated wink as he began to pull on his jumpsuit. "You do know what I mean, mate? I hear they got a girl at the Velvet . . . brunette hair trailing past her ass and if you pay her enough, she'll—"

Fritzi moved. He slammed the open locker door next to Stash's head and the other pulled his chin in, flushing a moment, the BOOM of the locker obscuring his last few words. Stash smiled slowly. "Well, now. Maybe you have other ideas of fun." He looked around at the gathering crowd, first shift who'd worked double time and second shift just coming off and joining them. "Do you know what Fritzi does for fun?"

"Stop it," Jack said.

But the man's sardonic gaze just passed over him. Nothing short of another fist in his mouth was going to stop Stash.

"Well, I'll tell you, mates. Fritzi spies on us for fun. Talks to the spider lady herself, he does. So if any of you are thinking of taking a long walk through a short tunnel, and maybe getting out of your contract a little early, don't discuss your plans in front of hill man here. He's a slaggin' spy, he is."

Jack shifted, but Boggs had caught his elbow and stopped him from moving. The older man whispered harshly in his ear, "Stash is right. Leave them alone. Got to let them work it out."

But Fritzi wasn't going to give Stash the opportunity. He lunged, quick on his feet for a big man, reminding Jack fleetingly of his old sergeant, and hit Stash hard enough to pick the man up off his feet and send him flying onto the floor. Miners scrambled out of the way and, as quickly, began to pick sides.

Fritzi wiped his mouth. "You talk about me any way you want—but you leave my daughter out of this—"

Stash looked up and blinked. "Dau—oh, you mean the brunette? Why, Fritzi, you should have told me. Then I could have told her. Jeezus, I might have gotten a discount!"

Fritzi never gave him a chance to get up. With a roar, he jumped the smaller man again.

Jack noticed, out of the corner of his eye, the camera lens of the security eye go red. A general alarm was on. He waded closer through the now cheering crowd. Fists jabbed the space around him as betting chits changed hands. But this fight wasn't like the one in the cafeteria, which had more or less dissolved into harmless haymakers for the hell of it.

No. Fritzi was going to kill Stash unless someone stopped it.

Jack mopped his forehead. He secured his towel

around his waist. The foot missing a couple of toes found the locker room floor slippery going. He lost his balance and a host of arms and hands helped him back to his feet even as he heard Stash give out a sick grunt and hit the bank of lockers like a side of meat. Fritzi picked up Stash and hung him on one of the doors, rested his slack arm in the next unit and slammed the door as hard as he could, even as the doors opened and the local Sweepers came pounding in, guns up and pointed. They'd had enough notice to put on riot gear. Or maybe they just slept in it.

"Freeze!"

The room froze, all except for Stash who sobbed and slumped to the floor as his jumpsuit tore away, his ruin of a hand sliding after him.

The Sweepers looked a bit ridiculous compared to the locker room audience, naked, half-naked and barely dressed. They looked about, helmet visors down, blackened out shields reflecting the miners' images back.

Pops grunted in the silence. "This is a lawful fight," he said, "We don't need you."

The foreman stepped in. His bullet head was sweaty and Jack wondered what he'd been interrupted at to come down here. He glared at Pops. "Anybody else say any different?"

No one spoke. Jack caught his breath, but then was unsure of what it was he was going to say. Stash might have been right about Fritzi's being a company spy, but who could blame Fritzi if they were holding his daughter in the company brothel?

Stash pulled himself to an upright position, leaning against the lockers. He licked swollen, purpled lips. "I claim the right to duel," he said, breathing heavily.

Fritzi straightened. He clamped his jaw shut, then opened it and said, "And I grant him the right." He looked down at the bloodied and mottled mess of Stash's right hand. "Since I'm the one who's been challenged, I say here and now."

Pops stirred. He looked at the foreman. "Mister Quade. They're requesting a duel. I say we give it to them. Settle bad blood and clear the air right now."

The foreman hunched his massive shoulders. "All right. I don't want to hear any more about it. You take care of it, Boggs, or I'm coming back to you." He pointed at the Sweepers. "We're out of here." They grouped and left, almost as impressively as they'd entered.

Stash looked surprised. "I didn't mean now . . ."

"Meaning what, Stash?" Pops looked down at him. "You asked for it."

"But I—I can't fight Fritzi like this." Stash gulped as he cradled his hand.

Boggs bent over him. He snorted. "Four days in sick bay'll take care of that. Get to your feet, boy. You made a challenge, now stick by it, or Quade'll have all our butts."

"I want a champion, then. Someone stick up for me. You all saw what Fritzi did to me when he had me down. C'mon. Somebody." Stash swayed on his feet, pale and trembling. "He'll kill me!"

A low voice jeered from the back of the room, "About time, mate."

The rest of the crew grumbled and shifted on their feet. A few of them, disinterested, turned away and reached into their lockers, to finish what they'd begun moments before. Stash was finally going to get all that he deserved.

Jack stepped out. "I'll do it."

CHAPTER 11

Boggs' attention swung toward Jack in disbelief. "You don't owe this gutter slag anything." Then he shrugged as Jack made no move. "Get dressed then. We'll pull the lockers back."

Stash gave Jack a weak grin and no one moved. "Thanks, mate."

"Don't thank me. I'm not doing it for you."

"Who then?"

"For Fritzi. He doesn't need a murder charge hanging around his neck." Jack took a look about the room, where he met startled face after startled face. He raised his voice. "Because we're all in this together, like it or not." Stash pulled in his chin, a faint sneer bringing the color back to his face. Jack went to his locker and dressed quickly, as the middle two rows were pulled back to create a kind of arena.

Fritzi had pulled a shirt over his head. He looked even more massive dressed than undressed, as the material puckered and strained over his body.

He looked at Jack. "I don't want to fight you, man."

Jack made a diffident movement. "You asked for a duel, too. Bad air's got to be settled, big man." He allowed himself a ghost of a smile. "You might be surprised." He slipped on his traction boots. The dead moon had a fairly close gravity norm, as it was an immense body, but even the ten percent it was off made for a certain hesitancy in movement. They all wore "grippers" to compensate.

He moved out and Fritzi stood, arms half open at his side, uncertain. Jack eyed the massive man and took stock of the fight he'd seen with Stash in the cafeteria as well as here in the lockers. This wasn't going to be any dance and punch exhibition. Fritzi only knew one way to fight and that was a massive, all-out launch of brute force and grappling.

The last thing Jack wanted was to be squeezed by those steel forearms.

Boggs pursed his lips. "He outreaches you, son," he called out. "Don't let him get ahold of you."

Jack circled Fritzi, never looking away, and answered, "Don't worry, Pops. I've got it covered." As if he were wearing the suit, he jumped, and his right foot lashed out, catching Fritzi neatly under the chin. The mountainous man staggered back with a cry of surprise and pain as Jack caught himself on landing.

Rubbing his jaw, Fritzi gave him a look, newly mingled with surprise and respect. "I didn't know you could do that," he said, in his childlike phrasing. Jack had a brief second in which to wonder if his daughter was like her father, not too brilliant and somewhat naive, when Fritzi roared and charged him.

Jack had reflexes he decided not to try to control, reflexes built into wearing the suit. He jumped, somersaulting out of Fritzi's way, letting the man's momentum carry him crashing into the lockers beyond. Before the calamitous noise filtered out, Jack had spun around and recoiled, ready for the next move. The miners crowded close now, calling to both of them, urging them on, and he began to hear odds and bets. Jack smiled thinly.

Fritzi backed out, shaking his head. He turned. He blinked. "What'd you do that for?"

Jack shrugged.

Fritzi waved a paw at him. "C'mon. Let me hit you right, so we can quit."

"No, Fritzi. We're not quitting on this one. Just like contracts, we've got to fight it through." Jack grinned. "But we can do it on our terms. We can both fight back."

Fritzi struck before he finished talking, jabbing with his right fist, and Jack dodged, but the blow clipped him. Jack's head snapped back. He dropped his shoulder and went on down, rolling with the blow so that most of the force went out of it. Fritzi's follow through left him wide open.

Jack threw a punch to his stomach as he got up, and then danced out of the way.

Fritzi never so much as grunted and his knuckles burned across the top. It'd been like punching a tunnel plate. Jack shook his head to keep his sandy hair from his eyes. Fritzi pivoted, amazingly light on his feet for one so massive, and Jack hesitated, seeing something in the man's movements he hadn't anticipated.

He stepped back quickly, but not quickly enough. Fritzi drove in, both fists hammering him. Red exploded along his chin and then in his own stomach and Jack staggered back. Fritzi was neither as muscle-bound nor stupid as he pretended, Jack's mind told him as his reflexes took over and brought him down, into a roll and then up again, out of range. There was something of the professional fighter in the way Fritzi had moved at him.

Jack was on his feet, though his vision had blurred and he blinked to clear it. Stash was yelling, "C'mon, mate, I've got a shift bonus on you! Get back in there!"

Fritzi smiled triumphantly. Jack wasn't sure he liked the light in the man's eyes.

Boggs wiped his nose and pushed him back toward his opponent. "You asked for it. Now get in there and get the matter cleaned up."

Jack's vision cleared just in time to focus on Fritzi's big ham of a hand swinging from way back, aimed at right between the eyes. Jack threw himself to the right, kicking his left knee as he went.

Fritzi grunted this time and doubled over the tiniest bit. Jack straightened and let him recover. The big man looked at him, dark eyes shining. "You're a good fighter."

"Thanks. You're not too bad yourself."

Fritzi's mouth twitched. "I was a champion before the gamblers got me." He drew his arms back into position. "Come a little closer."

Jack shook his head. "Not this time. Stash, what will it take for your honor to be satisfied?"

Stash spit pink foam onto the floor. "I want that big jerk stretched out cold."

Jack shook his head again. "Be reasonable."

"All right then. A good solid tag. To either one of you."

The New Aussie's fairness surprised Jack a little, but as he circled around Fritzi, staying out of reach, he noticed that Boggs had moved up behind Stash and appeared to be applying a little pressure of his own.

Pops called out. "Sounds fair. What about you, Fritzi?"

"All right, man." He beckoned to Jack. "I will hit you now."

Jack shook his head a third time. He barely had a split second to move while Fritzi did his damnedest.

And then he was very busy.

Fritzi abruptly dropped the pretense of boxing and moved in to grapple with him, clipping him before Jack could dodge, and he found himself contained by solid muscle that outweighed him by more than half his weight. He struggled to breathe and get loose, those priorities in strict order.

Fritzi said, breathing heavily in his ear, "I didn't tell you what I was champion *in*."

Jack used an elbow where it would do the most good, even as he dropped a shoulder and wiggled down out of the hold. He rolled over on the floor, gulped down a deep breath and gathered his muscles. Fritzi lunged again like some monster from out of deep water and Jack swam to stay out of reach. He got to his knees amidst shouts and warnings.

"Look out!"

Jack jumped. He leaped as if he'd hit the power vault in the suit. Fritzi grabbed empty air and tumbled, off balance.

It was the only opening Jack was likely to get. He reached out, righted the big man, and then swung.

Pain flared across his hand. The scar across his missing fifth finger went livid. Fritzi's head went back and his eyes glassed over. A mass of men behind caught him and set him back on his feet.

Before the big man's mouth could close, Pops moved in between them. "Done! Challenge met and over! Jack here's the winner."

Fritzi let out a shout. "Good man!" He charged Jack again, this time picking him up.

The world tilted and Jack looked down from Fritzi's shoulder. Spectators crowded in and around them as Fritzi carried him triumphantly into the barracks.

"Let me down," Jack said. Without warning, his colossal opponent did just that, and Jack disappeared in a sea of men.

One of them whispered at the back of his neck, "You're a dead man."

They helped Jack to his feet, crowding, bolstering him, shoving him good-naturedly into the barracks.

He had no way of knowing who'd spoken.

Stash stumbled into him and gave him a brotherly hug.

"I made back me fortune on you, mate!" he shouted above the noise.

Jack looked at him. "How's your hand?"

"Me hand? Oh, fine. Fine. A little plastiflesh, and it'll be right as rain."

"Will it?"

The noise quieted around the two men. The crowd, sensing something, drew back a little. Jack reached for, and captured against Stash's efforts, the injured member.

"A couple of bloodied knuckles. Why, I thought you were up for a cast, at the very least."

Stash shrugged and snatched his hand back. "Quick healer."

"No. No, you're not quick to heal at all. You've been setting us to fighting amongst ourselves since the day they thawed you out aboard ship. You're a scavenger, Stash. Get away from me and stay away." Jack took a deep breath. "The only way any of us can win is if we stick together. You're not a healer at all. You're a disease."

Stash's face flushed. He scrubbed his black hair from his forehead. The scarred eyebrow frowned deeply. "You'll be back, Jack," he said. "You all will. See, because you're like all honest men. Honest men don't like to do their own dirty work." He spat again from swollen lips. "But you'll always pay to have someone like me do it for you." He shoved his way through and disappeared out the barracks door.

Jack froze. He suddenly remembered where he had known Stash from. The man had washed out of the Guard program early on. And without a doubt, Stash had known him for what he was. What he didn't know now was what Stash would do with that information.

A man moved to go after Stash, saying, "It's after curfew, Pops."

Alfredo Boggs waved. "Let him go. There's nowhere for him to stay. He'll be back."

Thoughtfully, Jack watched him go. He only half-heard Fritzi say apologetically, "I'd like to tell you about my daughter sometime, man."

He turned. "That's all right, Fritzi. We've all got stories—and we've all got a lot of time together."

Or at least some of them did. Jack had no doubt now that his time was running short.

CHAPTER 12

The streets of Lasertown were a little closer to the sun and the stars than the tunnels—but not much. The dome screened off the direct radiation and it provided a grayed view of the sky. It was like being under a perpetual raincloud, Jack decided, as he stepped forth, Fritzi escorting him downtown. Even the deep velvet of unending space would have been preferable. The big man had kept up a steady stream of inconsequential talk. Jack half-listened as he looked around. The town was built on an industrial level, not there for the viewing of the eye or the lightening of the heart. That was part of its problems.

And the rest, he supposed, came from the people themselves. They jostled him rudely on the walkways as he transported from the mining center into the recreational/business sector where the shops were definitely open for business, but not happy about it. Their garish signs invaded the eyes, ears and even noses of the passersby, but there was no joy to be had here. No one in

Lasertown seemed to be there because they wanted to be.

Fritzi steered him to a small stand which was selling hot sandwiches. The man slapped the meat into a warm bun. Fritzi grinned like a kid as he picked up a bottle of pollen-yellow dressing and doused it, saying with his childlike enthusiasm, "This is great. There's nothing like it at the mess. Try some. You'll like it."

Jack had caught the sharp scent and shook his head. He took the proffered sandwich from the vendor and declined several of the other seasonings Fritzi suggested. The vendor took the money cheerlessly and looked away, sharp-eyed, for his next customer.

Jack took a bite of the sandwich. The meat was good, hot and savory, and its juices flavored the bread with all the dressing he needed.

"This is great, isn't it, Jack?" Fritzi said between gulps.

The vendor ignored them. His attitude irritated Jack. He took another bite. Fritzi dug his beefy fingers into a zipper pocket for more credit slips for another sandwich. Jack caught his elbow. "Let's try somewhere else, Fritzi. I don't think we're appreciated here."

Finally, the vendor looked at him. He was a squat, middle-aged man, with lines about his nondescript eyes. "Do us both a favor, kid, and move along. Take the walk somewhere. I'll get more business without miners around. Take my advice."

Fritzi frowned, but it was Jack who said, "What's wrong with miners?"

"Nothing. Absolutely nothing. You're a little smellier and poorer than the rest of us, but there's nothing wrong with that." The man glared at him. "Go back where you belong. At least you're underground there. If the Thraks hit here," and he waved a callused hand. "There's nothing between us and the Great Beyond but a cracked dome."

"You're blaming us for that?"

The vendor looked at him from purple shadowed, hallowed eyes. "Why do you think the Bugs are attacking? What, they want my sandwich stand? But they won't hit the mines direct. Why chance destroying what they're after? But the rest of us ... we're sitting targets and the blockade cuts our supplies every week. How would you like living like that?"

"You don't sound like you do."

"C'mon, Jack, let's go."

Jack shrugged off Fritzi's big paw. He looked the vendor in the eye. "So what's keeping you here?"

"Nothing. Nothing but poverty, son." The man laughed humorlessly. "I used to work the tunnels. I paid off my contract, with nothing left to go home on. Now I don't even know if I have a home. Now go on, get out of here. I've got to survive and won't anybody be coming around with you diggers here."

Fritzi steered Jack away from the vendor. "Don't make trouble, Jack," and he pulled them away from the stand. He sniffed at the fading savory aroma and added mournfully, "I didn't think you'd make trouble."

"I wasn't making trouble. I just wanted to know what he thought." Escapee contractors could expect little help or support from the domes. The slidewalk was crowded, but his companion's considerable bulk parted a wake around them. "Look at these people. None of them are smiling."

"People don't smile in Lasertown." Fritzi came to an abrupt halt, making about ten people trying to avoid him very unhappy. "I don't want you bothering Gail."

"Gail?"

"My daughter."

Now it was Jack's turn to steer Fritzi. "I won't make trouble for Gail, I promise."

"Good. Because she's a doper and sometimes she don't even recognize me . . . but I don't like it when she cries."

Silent for a few moments, Jack walked against the tide of people. "You're buying her out."

Fritzi nodded, the movement shrugging even his massive shoulders. "That's why I signed for five years. That'll get us both out."

If he lived that long. Five years in an operation like Lasertown was damn near a lifetime sentence. And that also explained why Fritzi maybe did a little company spying, to lighten that sentence. Jack didn't think Fritzi was smart enough to damage anybody by reporting them. Boggs had had the same opinion. Jack sighed.

Fritzi began his little monologue again, about everything in general and nothing in particular, until the streets converged and Jack saw that they had entered a region which excelled in promising noise and the ultimate fulfillment in life.

He was distracted for a moment from all the various kinds of fulfillment to be had by a pair of Walkers, their robes and under suits in somber colors contrasting with the cacophony of the pleasure sector. They walked briskly through the zone, obviously in transit somewhere and uncaring of the delights that surrounded them.

Fritzi made a noise, followed by, "Walkers."

Jack remembered the overheard conversation in the governor's office. He wondered briefly what the site must contain, to keep such a determined contingent of Walkers here to investigate it. Playing a waiting game in an outpost like this could become very expensive.

Fritzi came to an abrupt halt. "Here it is. We can go in here, or up the stairs."

"Here" led them through a voyeur pit and shop. Fritzi stopped at the arenas and looked hesitantly at him. Jack, although he was feeling particularly human, shook his head. "We're just visiting your daughter."

The unhappy look on Fritzi's face evaporated instantly. "I'm glad I brought you, Jack," he said, opening the door to the outside stairs.

Inside, the rooms were little more than boxes. Jack followed Fritzi hurriedly to the cell that belonged to Gail. She sat on the bed, and looked up when they came in, and her instantaneous smile was an echo of her father's expression. Fritzi found a chair to perch on and Jack sat on the floor next to the door.

She had been a pretty girl. Her lustrous brown

hair swung nearly to the floor. Her skin was a little too pale, and the roadmap of veins under the translucent skin was too purple. Her eyes misted a little as Fritzi leaned over and kissed her.

"How are they treating you, Daddy?"

He nodded. "Fair enough."

"Good." She looked apprehensively at Jack, then away quickly. "You make sure they feed you enough."

"I will." Fritzi looked across the hall and tore his eyes away, his rough skin reddening. Without turning around to look, Jack could tell from the noise that one of the girls was conducting a bit of business in the open.

Gail waved her palm over the locking beam and the door slid shut. Jack moved hastily as it threatened to take a nip out of his shoulder.

"You're not supposed to do that," Fritzi said.

"I know, but—" she looked at her hands. She'd knotted her fingers together uncomfortably.

Fritzi looked at Jack. "She's not supposed to do that," he repeated. "Unless she's got business."

Jack felt uneasy. "It's all right, " he said. "I'll leave her some money. You two just go ahead and visit."

She shot him a grateful look. The two of them talked for a few minutes while Jack leaned his head back against the door frame and rested.

They paused. Fritzi cleared his throat. "Well, daughter, that's about all this visit."

Gail brushed her long wings of hair from her slender face. "It's been good seeing you again. Don't stay away so long."

Her father looked at the floor. "I was here last week," he said, finally. "Don't you remember?"

That too pale skin pinked abruptly. Her eyes misted over. Fritzi reached over, rumbling, "Now don't do that."

Gail blotted her eyes. "Right." She sniffed. "Now I've got something to tell you. Something's going on, I don't know what. One of the girls is missing—well, I guess she's not missing any more. They found her body outside the domes."

Jack straightened. "The sleeping sickness?"

She nodded. "They think so. I hear she turned all weird before she left. Said she could hear voices calling her."

"Did you know her?"

"Only a little. She was all right."

"Was she—could she have been taken out by someone?"

Gail shook her head. "They don't think someone did that to her. A camera caught a couple of shots of her, alone." She gave a tiny shudder. "Daddy, they're doing some work at the site. No one's supposed to know about it. They're using some of the old crew—told them they'd get off early if they worked the site." Her eyes misted heavily. "They might ask you because they know you need the credits. Don't go! It's . . . it's dangerous and ugly out there. I've heard some terrible things. They say that's where the sickness is worse. Don't let them make you go!" Her voice went high and strained and Fritzi grabbed her in a ferocious bear hug.

"I won't leave you alone," he promised.

Jack got up and waited outside as they said

good-bye. He counted out a few of his precious recreational credits. He pushed them into Gail's hand as they left. As they walked back through, Jack felt an urgent and burning need, but knew this was not the place where he could satisfy it. Why was Franken bearing the cost and danger of excavating the site instead of turning it over to the Walkers? And did it, maybe, have something to do with the Thrakian interest in Lasertown? Norcite ore was valuable, but was it worth breaking the treaty over? He frowned as he thought about it, and as he returned to the tunnels, the unhappiness on his face mirrored all that he'd found in the domes of Lasertown.

A mournful wail drifted through the barracks and the mess. It seemed to permeate the mood and even the snap of cards and click of dice did little to disperse it. Boggs looked up once, rubbed the back of his neck, and said, "I wish he'd choke on that mouth sync."

Equally perverse, Stash said, "I like it. Deal."

They returned to their card game.

Jack sat over a plastiboard, sketching out what he could remember of the city from the governor's offices and from his trip with Fritzi. Fritzi sat across the table from him, happily eating biscuits and what passed for milk from the automat. He seemed to be blissfully unaware of what Jack was doing with the sketchboard, but even if he reported Jack, he doubted the information would pique anyone's interest. Bull Quade's Sweepers picked up much more flagrant information over the wiretaps throughout the barracks, if anyone even bothered to monitor them.

He rubbed his temple thoughtfully. Almost as if called forth by his unconscious, the mess door schussed open and Quade stood in its shadows, looking about the mess. The squat, bald man looked more tired than mean, for once, Jack thought as he lifted his head to stare back.

"Boggs."

Summoned, the shift supervisor looked up.

"Spread the word. We want a crew for some work outside the tunnels and domes. Triple overtime for any who volunteer."

"Outside the tunnels?"

"It's risky, that's why the money's good." Bull nodded sharply. "Send 'em to me."

Fritzi slowly came to attention. He hesitated, then shrugged his massive shoulders. "I'll go."

Jack reached for him. "Fritzi! You promised Gail—"

He shrugged Jack off. "What kind of work?"

"Digging."

The mournful music broke off, and the shuffling of feet from the barracks to the other end of the mess began, as off-duty crew pressed in to hear what was going on.

"What happened to the old crew?"

"Everyone gets tired. Plus, the shift bosses were raising hell with me that I wasn't givin' everybody the opportunity to earn that kind of credit."

"Bullshit," an anonymous voice heckled. "The work's as dangerous as hell."

Quade raised his voice. "All of you. Either

volunteer or don't. I ain't here to baby-sit you. Make up your minds."

The colossal man stepped toward Quade. "I'm in," Fritzi said.

No one else moved. There was a deathly silence as the foreman and Fritzi left, and someone whispered, "That'll be the last we see of him."

No one disagreed.

CHAPTER 13

Amber wound her hands tightly together. She missed the constant thrumming of the ship, though not its movement, and the docking had been anything but smooth—something about an evasive pattern. She bit her lip. She could do anything but wait. Anything.

The Lasertown accommodations were anything but plush even though it was obvious the best that could be gotten had been reserved for Colin. The Walkers stationed here on the moon had been coming by in a steady stream to pay their respects and talk to their leader. She had sat in the side room, watching their faces illuminated with wolfish hunger as they'd waited for their audience. She was not sure what it was that had made Colin a saint, but she sensed that his followers believed in it with all their heart.

Which made the Walker far different from any religious figure she'd ever known on the streets of Malthen. Religion and parapsychology were two of the biggest scams that could be run. Gambling was a scam, too, but it was always there and anyone who gambled knew that there were winners and losers. But religion was different. It never preached losers. Amber's lip curled slightly. She'd yet to see any winners come out of those scams.

But it was patently obvious, even with her cynical outlook and inexperience, that this man was something different. Walkers were radicals. They didn't worry about a Second or Third Coming. They weren't looking for God's boundaries—they were looking for His limitless horizons. Everywhere He could, and had, touched.

St. Colin exuded a quiet kind of magnificence. Perhaps it was his deep-rooted faith or his intelligence or his ability to organize people to do almost anything he asked of them. Whatever it was, he had it and he wasn't the sort of man to abuse it. She'd been surprised when she found out that Jack had worked for St. Colin in an internal matter at the Emperor's request. She hadn't heard anything about that. But then, Jack had stopped talking to her much. He'd not visited very often that last month, what with her school schedule and his duty schedule. The corner of her mouth quirked. School had certainly gone down the Disposall. She hadn't thought of it in weeks.

St Colin had agreed with her that Pepys shouldn't be contacted until Jack was positively ID'd and located, but even then the Emperor would probably not be able to pull strings. Pepys prided himself on impartiality. He could help Jack once Jack had begun to extricate himself, but not before. Not for a paltry matter like contract labor. Galactic war was another matter.

One which Jack was likely to start once she got the armor to him. Amber gave a thin smile. She folded her hands neatly in her lap, determined to wait in the hotel until St. Colin's return. He had promised her he would find out Jack's whereabouts and arrange a meeting. Even contract labor had some privileges. A visit from family would be in order, once he was off shift. Then it was only a matter of getting a copy of his contract and seeing how he'd been signed, chilled and delivered. She'd find the loopholes. And if she couldn't ... perhaps a little psychic persuasion would help.

The enigmatic smile stretched wider. Amber felt her search was almost over.

The hotel door vibrated and she sensed Lenska and the Walker returning. It schussed open in response to their palms and she sprang to her feet in welcome.

St. Colin was frowning. He crossed the room and held out his hands to her. "Patience, Amber."

"Did you find him?"

"Yes, but ..." and he looked down at her with those brown eyes of his that had already searched quite a few solar systems for some sign of his savior. "There's been an accident."

"What?" She flinched in alarm, but he held her solidly. "What kind of accident?"

"In the mining tunnels. They're doing all they can. They'll call us when they know."

* * *

Jack pulled the deepsuit off the rack. The tech, Renaldo, grinned at him from the other side. "Double shift again?"

"Whatever it takes." He smiled back. "You guys got it easy. You stay back in here and sit around all day—"

Renaldo fairly beamed under the ribbing. He waved his prosthetic arm at Jack. "That's right, digger. You go work out there where the air is real thin. I'll stay here and take a nap." He ducked his head as one of the cable layers yelled at him, and went over to see what was wrong.

Jack stepped into the suit. The feeling that it was the same as his armor and yet entirely different always set him on edge. It was a suit, yes, but flimsy and unworthy of him. He gritted his teeth as he wired and tubed himself and then shrugged the rest of the suit on. Reaching for his helmet, he stifled a yawn. Double shifting took its toll sooner or later and he'd begun to feel it deep in his bones. Carefully he looked over his indicators and readouts. The techs had given the suit a full charge. Today he could walk out, if he wanted, but there would be no place to go. He stretched to limber his neck muscles, thinking that even if he had found a place to go, doubling back to the domes, he'd be picked up immediately unless there was another Thrakian raid and he could be counted among the missing. The timing was delicate and almost entirely out of his control.

But not always. It would not always be beyond his ability. Jack pulled the helmet on and twisted it into locking position.

Instantly the noise and bantering of the rest of the crew suiting up was muffled away. Ron was teasing Dobie again. He could hear them vaguely, but it was as though he'd been shut away into a silent world where one was measured by deed, not talk. It was a world in which he felt comfortable, though not all of the laborers did. He left the com lines off.

Stash shouldered past him wordlessly as he headed for the trams. Jack watched him go. Alfredo Boggs tapped him on the shoulder and leaned forward so their face plates could touch.

"I want you to work the T-section tunnel today."

He nodded. Satisfied, Boggs backed away and led the way to the trams. Jack climbed aboard, bulky now that his suit had pressurized, and settled down at the back. His would be one of the last stops as he'd be working on the farthest and newest section. Even Crew One hadn't been in there yet. The tram dropped him off, then pulled away without letting another welder off and Jack watched, baffled.

He chinned on the com. "Hey, Pops—where's Fritzi?"

There was no answer. Jack watched out his face plate. He pursed his lips, wondering if he should be concerned, then shrugged and began walking to the work station. It was a common safety factor to never isolate a worker. They always went at least in twos, sometimes in bigger teams. But the work schedule was running behind and Boggs might be stretching a little to cover lost time. He hadn't spotted Fritzi in the shop. Maybe he hadn't come back in from the site yet.

Working alone, it would take most of first shift to finish the welding on the one arm and most of the second shift on the second joint. He wouldn't be able to request test pressurization until tomorrow when he or someone else finished the job. The tunnels were never left pressurized beyond the barracks bulkheads, but it was common practice to test them, in case something happened on the upper levels or in the domes and the population had to be evacuated down here. Even so, the recycling computers monitored the airworthiness of the tunnels carefully. If any of the sections lost integrity, the bulkheads at either end would shut down immediately and seal it off. It was the only way to prevent a chain reaction of leaks that could jeopardize all of Lasertown.

The tunnels encompassed most of the veins that were considered worth mining. Occasionally an operation was set up beyond the bulkheads, through a membrane which reduced some of the hazard but still left a miner outside. Those operations were worked only if the profit was worth the extreme risk. Working in deepsuits inside the tunnels was risky enough. If a suit should blow or a tunnel collapse, a miner was damned near doomed, anyway.

The lights flickered. Jack looked up and saw the gray mountain of a man wavering toward him. He chinned the com on. "Hey, Fritz! How's it going? Looks like it's just the two of us today."

The big man nodded, but the com lines stayed

empty and open. Jack touched his arm and, standing on tiptoe, touched face plates as Fritzi bent over. His face was shadowed, but Jack pulled back, stunned. It was as though he'd looked at a man twenty years older than his friend, at a face overwritten with the heavy gullies and lines of dissipation.

"Are you all right?"

Fritzi gave an impatient, jerking nod.

"All right. Just asking." Jack reached to his belt hook and unlatched the welding wand. "I'll take this seam."

Automatically, Fritzi moved to the other side. In a few seconds, his wand flared to life and the two of them worked silently.

Jack lost himself in the orange-red line of welding as the seams came together and melded at his touch. He'd been working for hours when he realized that someone was talking, quietly, steadily, nonsensically.

It was Fritzi.

Jack turned the wand off and looked around. Fritzi had been moving methodically down the seams on his side, but the man in the gray suit moved in herky-jerky motions as though he fought every move he made.

Jack's mouth went dry. He licked his lips, swiveled his head, found the drinking nipple and wet his mouth. He forced his voice to stay casual. "Fritzi! How's it going?"

The suit spasmed to attention and turned in his direction. Jack fought a wild memory of battle armor with berserkers exploding out of them and his heart went into a wild palpitation that he breathed deeply to calm. This was *Fritzi*, for god's sake. And Lasertown, not Milos.

But, for all his efforts to stay quiet, he knew that something had gone terribly wrong. Fritzi had not spent half a shift welding seams shut. Instead, he'd been cutting them open.

Fritzi stood in front of him, convulsing like a man gone mad, and the com lines signal broke apart in wild static.

He heard only, "I've got to go!" then nothing but the crackle of his own lines as Fritzi turned and ran, head first, at an unwelded seam. If he burst through that, there was nothing but dead rock beyond.

And the force of the erupting tunnel could well tear him and Jack apart.

"Wait! Fritzi, no! Don't!" Jack dove at the man's ankles, but Fritzi's weight carried them careening into the weakened section.

It held. God knew how or why, but it held. Fritzi rolled over in his grip and Jack could hear muffled sobbing. He curled his hand into a fist and rapped gently on the face plate.

"Turn on the com, Fritzi."

The crackle in his ears returned. Fritzi swallowed in great, heaving gulps. Jack helped him to sit up.

"What is it? What's wrong?"

"Ahhhhh." The man rocked back and forth in grief. His gloved hands went up to hold his helmet.

"Is it Gail?"

The rocking figure stopped, then twisted toward him. Through the screening, he could see Fritzi's face, grown red and bilious from all his emotion. Then, slowly, he shook his head.

Jack sat back. "What is it, Fritzi? Come on, this is Jack. You can tell me."

Without a word, the man bounded up and charged across the T-section. Jack jumped to his feet, too, surprised by the explosion of energy. Fritzi hammered at the tunnel. "Let me out! Let me out!"

"Fritzi! Dammit, listen to me! What is it?" Then Jack changed his tone. "I can help you get out, if you tell me."

The colossal being in the bunched up deep-suit slowly turned toward him. Jack heard a sharp intake of breath over the com lines. He held his own. Was Fritzi going to lunge at him or talk with him?

Fritzi exhaled, a long quavering sigh. He dropped to his knees. "I went out," he said, in gusty, wavering words that were almost too low for Jack to hear. "They took us out to dig. And it . . . it was there, Jack. It was waiting for me. Just me."

"What was there?"

"What they wanted us to dig for. It's . . . it's underground. It can't be seen yet. But I've got to go back, to help it. It . . . calls me. All the time. Sometimes I can stand it, but—" and he broke off and began sobbing again.

Jack, for lack of anything better to do, thumped Fritzi's shoulder. "It'll be all right," he said. He wondered if something ungodly was alive, waiting in the depths of the dead moon.

"I've got to go!" Fritzi screamed. He knocked

Jack aside as he got to his feet and barreled toward the weak section again. A second time, Jack dove and caught his friend by the ankles as Fritzi hit the tunnel with a resounding thud.

It held, Fritzi lay facedown, temporarily exhausted. Jack was reaching for the long-range com switch when the explosion went off. The world opened up and rock powdered around him. He hit, still clutching Fritzi by the ankles, and a mountain fell on top of them.

CHAPTER 14

The first thing Jack noticed when he woke was that his gloves were empty. He flexed his hands, remembering the solid feel of Fritzi's heavily muscled body within his grip, and wondered where the man had gone. And then he noticed that his hands were about the only thing he could move, that half of Lasertown must be resting on his back.

Why had the tunnel blown? Fuzzily, he remembered hearing the sound of an explosion.

He held his breath and listened for the deathly sound of a telltale leak. Nothing came to his ears but the normal hum of the suit's systems. He seemed to be intact. So far. He was blind, nearly, for his face plate pointed downward and this suit had no cameras for odd angle viewing like his armor did. Jack lay very still and tried not to think of his odds . . . or Fritzi's. Had the man been torn away from him by the avalanche of rock? Or had he clawed his way up and through and out? This particular tunnel followed

173

a vein relatively close to the moon's surface. Fritzi could have made it.

But to what fate? Fritzi had about as much chance wandering around up there as he did buried down here. Maybe less.

He couldn't see his hands. The weight on the back of the suit kept him facedown and blind, but slowly, determinedly, he dragged his arms back. He could feel the gravel shift and pull at him. He'd been buried like this once before, in a couple of tons of silt and river water.

Then it was the battle armor that had gotten him out. Now he had nothing to depend on but the recycling computers' sensors and his fellow diggers. There would be an alarm and a crew. Any second now, he should be hearing Boggs' gravelly voice over the com letting him know they were going to get him out.

Jack shifted his head, turtlelike and nudged the com switch to make sure it was still on. Nothing. Not even break-up. Was it functioning? Why wasn't anybody trying to reach him?

"This is Jack, Boggs. I'm down in the T-section. We've had a blow-out. I know the bulkheads are probably sealed off, but I'm alive and in good shape. Somebody come get me."

He managed to pull his hands back and tucked them under his face plate. There was no more grinding of shifting rock. A portion of the tunnel must be curving over him, protecting him from most of the rock fall, shielding him even as it kept him imprisoned on the tunnel flooring. As long as there was no leak in his suit, and he had air, he could hold out.

The second thing that struck him was that this had been no accident. Boggs' pairing of Jack with Fritzi was deliberate, even though Fritzi's aberrant behavior must have been apparent. Why? Why would Boggs want to take Jack out? Was it Boggs who'd whispered in Jack's ear that he was a dead man?

And the third thing that struck him was that nothing that had happened in the last twenty or so years had been an accident, except perhaps for the survival of the transport cold ship with him still alive inside it. He hadn't been meant to live, not on Milos, not on Claron, not on Malthen and certainly not here.

And the fact that he'd remained alive was not due to his alert grasp of the facts. He'd stumbled along on luck and fortune, not willing to believe that he'd really been a target, convinced that he was too insignificant to be the cause of a firestorm that had destroyed an entire planet.

He looked into the dead dirt grinding into his faceplate. "Amber," he said quietly to himself, "I think they finally kicked the farm out of the farm boy."

This was war. He knew it now, as he should have known it all along. Not between the Thraks and the Dominion or any one of the dozens of other combinations he'd been juggling. It was war between him and Winton. Why, he wasn't sure. But who and what Jack was, was important enough to a galactic empire to wipe out an entire planet. Jack saw it now, crystal clear, as he'd never seen it before. It was war, and he was a soldier in it, whether he had his armor or not.

It was time he started thinking like it.

Static trickled in over his com lines. Jack turned his head. The volume was greatly damped down. It was difficult in his current position, but he skewed his head around so he could check the power gauges. Air, he had plenty of. Battery power seemed to be another matter. Any signals he was putting out or receiving were fading and rapidly. He had some sort of drain, possibly a short. That kind of damage meant he probably had a leak, too, but the suit had an inner layer, a self-sealant, which could hold a small leak for a while. The good news was that he hadn't noticed a leak. Either it had sealed or the suit damage didn't include a puncture. The bad news was, if his suit ran out of charge, it made relatively little difference.

Sound bled in over the static. Jack twitched. Was that Boggs he heard? Or Bull Quade's voice?

Never mind. Anybody's would do.

His throat had gone dry as he croaked back, "Here. Down here. Follow the signal."

He chinned the emergency switch to put out an automatic signal, had a moment to notice how stale the air had gotten, and realize how terribly, terribly sleepy he was and then, nothing.

Amber held onto St. Colin's arm, quivering imperceptibly, telling herself it was the chill of the sight of the tunnel mouths opening up into the domes like some hungry, parasitic creature that swallowed men whole. She heard, though she wasn't meant to, one of the foremen saying softly, "They're bringing the bodies up now."

Bodies? Jack? She curled her fingers tighter onto the Walker's arm as he cleared his throat and answered. "How many?"

"Five got caught. Two different sections blew out."

"Chain reaction?"

"No. At least, we don't think so. And one man is missing."

"Missing?"

"He's not where he should be. It looks like . . . like he just got up and walked away."

Colin patted her hand absently as he answered, "Inside the tunnels?"

"No. He's outside somewhere."

Lenska muttered, "Good as dead, then." He made a funny sound and then added, "I'm sorry, Amber."

She looked up fiercely. "He's not dead! I'd know it if he was."

Colin kept his big, warm hand over her chilled one this time and squeezed it gently. "Patience. It might not even be Jack," he chided. "They won't let us down in the mining operation or the barracks. Let's be thankful they're letting us wait in the loading docks."

Amber said nothing. She turned her fierce gaze elsewhere, to the tram cars waiting to take the dead and injured to the hospital. Men sitting around, bored looks on their faces, waited to hear. Suddenly, there was a buzz of activity. They got to their feet and began to make arrangements of the litters and medical supplies. "They're coming," she said, and the hoarseness of her voice surprised her.

The foreman standing with them listened to his ear plug and then nodded sharply. "They're on the elevator," he said, "with the first load." He looked at the two Walkers and the girl. "At least one of 'em's alive."

"Who is it? Did they say who it was?"

He shook his head and walked away, busy directing a tram car into position by the elevator shaft.

Amber could not stop trembling. Her throat ached for the long moments it took for the elevator to rise into position and the freight bay doors to open. When they did, it was with a siren frenzy of sound and movement.

"Coming through, move it, move it, move it!"

She saw broken bodies, blood and flesh leaking out from shreds of deepsuits, men and gear melded forever. An oxygen tank and mask obscured the face of one man, hidden under a mylar blanket, his gurney propelled forward by a team of men. Amber broke loose from St. Colin and surged forward. She ducked between the paramedics and forced her way to the gurney, stopping it.

She didn't recognize him. One of the medics snapped at her, "Get out of the way," and she answered petulantly, "I just want to know who it *is*."

The nearly motionless man moved. His head turned. Under the clear plastic oxygen mask that obscured nearly as much as it revealed, pale blue eyes opened. Then he croaked, "Amber?"

"Oh, my god," she said and fell to her knees in tears.

"It should have been much worse than it was," the doctor said, moving away. "He'll be bruised around the knees for a while, but he'll be up and around tomorrow. The only thing that got to him was the bad air, but his suit was functioning on a minimal level. I don't foresee any long-term effects." He spoke, not to the patient or Amber, but to the Walker. "We'll have him back in the barracks in the morning."

Amber's back tensed. The doctor's voice held an undertone, as though he was pronouncing the fact that the garbage would be back in the Disposall in the morning—where it belonged. She held onto Jack's hand. It had been months, she knew, but her throat stayed convulsively tight. He looked awful. He'd lost so much weight and muscle tone, and his skin had gone deathly pale. She wondered if he'd be strong enough to wear the battle armor. Strong enough physically as well as mentally. But she kept her thoughts to herself. Jack didn't even know she had Bogie with her, yet.

The Walker waited until the doctor left the cubicle and then sat down with a flourish of his deep blue robe. He looked about cautiously and the corner of Amber's mouth twitched. The religious leader was looking for monitors. He was not, she noted, quite the innocent he made himself out to be.

"Well, my boy," Colin said blandly. "It gives me great pleasure to return a favor."

"Me, too," Jack said dryly. "How long before you have me out of here?"

"The governor assures me a couple of days, no longer. Quite an unusual woman," he added as an afterthought.

Amber winced as Jack made a feeble attempt to smile. "Watch out for her," he husked.

"Oh, I will, have no doubt." St. Colin returned the smile. "My men have been sitting here for months trying to deal with Governor Franken."

Jack struggled to sit up. Colin protested, but Amber helped. The effort brought a faint rush of color to his too pale face. His sandy blond hair was dirty and grimed. She tucked a strand away from his eyes. In the morning, they'd promised him a shower as though it had been a gift. Perhaps it had been.

"How did you find me?" This to St. Colin, but the Walker's wise brown gaze flicked to Amber where it held steady.

"You'll have to ask her. I have the feeling that I only come in toward the end of the tale." He gathered up the plastifile. "I have some work to do, if you don't mind. I'll be back later." He paused at the cubicle door. "Don't stay too long, Amber. Beep Lenska when you want to go back to the hotel."

"All right."

Jack's gaze watched the Walker leave, before he turned back to her.

"Don't ask," Amber said faintly.

"All right. I won't." He fussed at the oxygen tubes about his nose. "Did you find out who did it?"

"He's dead. He was supposed to have you picked up and terminated, but he decided to make a little more money, so he had you chilled down and contracted out. The trail was very well hidden."

"Who was he?"

"Huan Ng. I wasn't able to trace him backward, but I think we both know . . ." the sentence trailed off.

Jack closed his eyes briefly.

"Jack?"

"I'm all right." He looked back at her.

"You're supposed to rest. Maybe I can catch up with Colin."

He put up his hand. She looked at it, remembering suddenly that she'd forgotten about the sheared off little finger, and she caught his hand, warming it between hers. "Don't go yet."

She settled into her chair a little happier. "All right. I won't."

"What about Fritzi? No one will tell me about Fritzi."

Amber frowned slightly as she thought. "Is he the miner supposed to have been buried with you?"

"Yes."

She shrugged, a lithe movement that echoed throughout her supple body, giving Jack thoughts that shocked him. He pinked up, but she didn't seem to notice his sudden flush. Had he been gone that long that she'd grown up that much?

"I don't know about anybody else. One guy lived through it, but he lost both legs. He'll be shipped out for prosthetics. And then there's the guy they won't really talk about—"

Quickly, "Won't talk about?"

"Yeah. Somebody evidently just got up and walked out. But he's supposed to be outside."

"Outside?"

"You know." Amber shivered, in spite of herself. "Outside."

"That's got to be Fritzi." Jack rolled the information over in his mind. The suit, if it hadn't sustained damage, would still have enough supplies. Fritzi could still be alive. But he wouldn't stay that way much longer. He eyed the clock on the wall. They would be coming off first shift about now. From about now, Fritzi was running on borrowed time.

"What is it?"

He rubbed his forehead wearily. "Nothing. I'm just going to close my eyes for a few minutes—I don't sleep long, remember? So don't go away. I want you here when I wake up." The numbing sensation of the sedatives he'd been given swept through him. He ought to call Boggs or somebody and tell them where he thought Fritzi'd probably gone. Problem was, he couldn't decide if the miner was better off wandering off or not. By the time he'd decided, he was sound asleep.

"We want you out on first shift, whether you ship out tomorrow or not," Boggs said. He hesitated, then held a hand out to Jack. "Good to have you back."

"Did you find Fritzi?"

"No, but based on your information, we should. We found where he dug through the other side from the blow-out." Boggs, hesitated, frowning, his nose and ear hairs bristling in unease. He rubbed a hand over his smooth head. "Jack, I'm sorry. I thought you could keep a handle on him. When they'd sent him back from the dig saying he was causing problems and they couldn't use him, I thought he was going to be all right. And I figured you could keep the lid on if he wasn't."

So now Jack knew why Fritzi'd been paired with him. He felt a wave of remorse. "What happened?"

"We don't know. We found a third charge that didn't go off. It looks like someone deliberately sabotaged the tunnels. We've never been hit like that before."

"Inside or outside?"

The wizened man looked at him. "What?"

"Were the charges inside or outside?"

"Outside."

Jack pondered the possibilities. That meant that someone who could leave the domes had done it, and most miners couldn't get out once above ground if their lives depended on it. The same conclusion dawned on Boggs' face.

"Why?"

He shrugged."Damned if I know. If Fritzi hadn't been trying to cut his way out and weakened the tunnel, the force of the pressure blowout would have done us in, too. In retrospect, we were lucky." And, in retrospect, someone had to have known those sections were being pressure tested that shift. Unless, of course, someone just wanted minor damage done instead of the havoc that was wreaked.

"Shit, Jack," Boggs said. "I'm just a goddamn

contractor and miner. This stuff is getting too heavy for me. What with the site and all—" he stopped and clamped his thin lips together, having said more than enough.

Jack half-smiled. "Got another suit for me?"

"It's on the racks." Whatever else Boggs wanted to say to him was drowned out by the crew coming in from the mess to suit up.

Stash strode across the hall, his winged eyebrow up in astonishment.

"Mate! You're back on contract with us?"

He shook his head. "Only for a shift or two."

"Lucky, that's what you are. I always said you was my lucky charm." But the look in Stash's dark eyes didn't match the tone of his voice. Jack felt uneasy. He felt his bruised back pummeled by good-natured slaps as his fellow workers grabbed for his hand. The clamor of their voices rose and then fell as the com system crackled on.

"Woman on the floor. Woman on the floor."

"Jeez," said Perez. "What's happening now?" The cable worker shrugged aside from Jack as visitors crowded into the barracks.

He should have known it would be Amber. She shouldered her way through, her face pinched up tight the way it got when she was very unhappy or cold or, in his case, he thought as she hugged him tightly, both. Whistles and calls drowned out what she said first, but then he heard, "The hospital didn't bother to let me know you'd gone!"

"I'm still contracted here."

St. Colin had made his way through, too. The

rough cross on his chest still swung a little from the rhythm of his vigorous stride. "You're going out on shift?"

"Have to. Until Franken brings the word down."

"Don't go."

Jack loosened her grip around his neck a little. "Have to," he repeated. "If I don't, they have the right to force me. You wouldn't like what they can do as coercion. Besides, I want to work on the blow-up. They haven't found Fritzi yet."

Colin pursed his lips. "I don't think it would be wise for anyone to go out. I have word that the Thraks are changing position this morning. Opinion has it they're coming in for another strafing run. With the tunnel network already damaged . . ." his voice trailed off.

Amber had already given in. She said, "Well, if you've got to go, then I've got a surprise for you." She pointed across the barracks to Lenska who was struggling to wheel in a large trunk.

Jack recognized the trunk right away. Its presence rocked him. The barracks quieted as Colin's beanpole of an aide set it up and opened it, pulling out the portable rack inside.

Stash let out a low whistle as the white battle armor gleamed in the barracks' half-light. "Well, now, mates," he said. "You're going to see just what this here man is made of."

Boggs scratched his head. "What's going on, Jack?"

Stash prodded some more. "Not just Jack, is

it, anymore. No, blokes, you're in the presence of Captain Jack Storm ... currently commissioned in the Emperor's Guard, he is. One of the newly reformed Dominion Knights. That's his bloody armor."

Jack half-heard him, drawn by the armor. He was out of the crowd before he knew it, only Amber by his side, as he reached for it. He could almost see the painted out insignia gleaming on its chest. His fingertips brushed the armor.

Hi, boss!

"Suit up," Amber urged.

"In that thing?" Boggs' gravelly voiced followed them. "That's a one-man tank!"

Jack looked over his shoulder. "You'll need some fire power to clear out the T-section, right? And that's where Fritzi went out, right?"

"Well, yeah, but—"

Cutting him off and ignoring him, Jack said to Amber, "Is he charged?"

"Yeah and revvin' to go."

"All right." He peeled off his shirt, not hearing her soft cry of dismay at his bruised torso, and reached for the armor, hands pulling at the intricate seam. Bogie fell open, welcoming him.

It seemed to take an eternity, suiting up. The armor was heavy and demanding, much more demanding of him than the deepsuit. But he did it, even up to the helmet, dropping it on and then screwing it into place. Bogie wrapped around him with a powerful and exultant embrace.

Jack put his head back to let out an unrestrained shout of power and joy—but the noise never left his throat.

The tunnels reverberated with the sound of alarm klaxons and men scattered.

CHAPTER 15

Jack tore off his helmet. "Get them into suits," he yelled at Boggs, but the crew was already stampeding toward the shop, as the walls shook and the force of a blast echoed down them. He grabbed Amber by the wrist and she cried out in pain before he remembered his capability in the armor and softened his grip. Colin and Lenska wavered behind him.

"We've got to get out." The aide quailed.

"Better off in here. The mining operation is rarely hit," Jack told him. "But you'll need a suit if the bulkheads get sealed off."

His ears popped. The worst he could figure on must be happening. "Hurry! We've got no time to lose."

The doors between the barracks and the shop began to close, the sealing rims in place. He pushed Colin and Lenska through, but caught Amber back just before she'd have been cut in two.

They stood alone in the barracks.

"What's happening?"

"The circulation pumps have either been hit, or there's been major damage to the tunnels."

"How do we get out?"

Jack pivoted. The corridor to the mess was already sealed off. He smiled grimly. "We go the hard way. But it'll be better down in the tunnels until the raid's over."

"But—" Amber paled. "What about me?"

He looked down at her, gathering his senses, even as Bogie began to rage. He would walk through walls if he had to. Could walk through walls. Bogie engulfed him as he never used to. Jack shrugged. The suit, once custom fitted to his body, felt almost cavernous.

"Jack?"

His ears popped again. The barracks was either losing air or being shut down by the recycling computers. He reached for her.

"You're in this with me," he said, and opened a seam to pull her in with him.

It was not so much that she was riding piggyback, but that she'd been bound to him by the suit, both of them wedged in. He lost the ability to reach one or two of the internal switches because she was in the way or blocking his head movement, but the arrangement would do, for now. It was either that or leave her in the barracks with a steadily dwindling air supply. The double doors of the shop defied entrance at the moment even if he could get her that far.

Amber panted in his ear.

"Relax. We've got enough air for both of us," Jack said, wondering how long the situation would last.

"It's—not that." She shivered.

He felt every contour of her body along his bare torso. The fact reminded him keenly that Amber wasn't exactly a little girl anymore.

"What's wrong?"

"It's Bogie," she whispered. "He—it's so strong!"

And the berserker rage filling him at that moment was overwhelming. The creature was incredibly fierce in his joy at having Jack and Amber both within his sphere. Jack had been enjoying the adrenalin rush, being pumped up to do whatever he was going to do next. He'd forgotten her heightened sensibilities and told Bogie to back down.

But boss—

Jack pushed. The flood of emotions subsided a little. Amber's slender arms about his neck tightened as he leaned into motion.

"Where are we going?"

"Not into the shop. It's been sealed off and if I break through, I'll ruin the integrity of the area. The barracks is already having problems, so I won't be adding to the leak or the damage by leaving. We'll circle round and meet the tunnels at the shop exit." Even as Jack talked, he savored the strength of the armor. He cocked his fist and pointed a gauntlet finger. The answering ray melted down the seal. Then he kicked his way through, Amber gasping in his ear.

"What about Colin?"

"Let's hope he's seen the inside of a deepsuit

before. If they're not panicked, the crew's a good sort and they'll help." Jack surveyed the corridor. Vaguely, like an ear-popping shove, he felt another shock wave. Reflexively, he looked up. The Thraks were merciless this time. He wondered if the main domes were being hit.

And why.

He surveyed his cameras and turned on his heel, heading downward.

"Where are we going?"

"Down. One way or another."

He stopped outside what had been the shop and the little tram car station to the various tunnels.

"Oh, my god," Amber whispered over his shoulder.

The lights flickered and in their place, the helmet laid down a wide beam across the operations area. It had taken nearly a direct hit, down one of the elevator shafts. The Thraks weren't avoiding the mines this time. The shop doors were blown open, metal and plastic peeled back, and inside he could see suits and bodies thrown about. His suit gauge gave an air reading back to him and he knew without going into the damaged room that whoever was in there had not survived unless they'd been suited and hadn't been shrapneled. He felt Amber bury her nose at the back of his neck.

"What about Colin?" she asked, her voice muffled. It made a moist tickle that he wanted to scratch but couldn't reach.

Now we fight. Bogie said.

"Damn right."

"What?" asked Amber.

"Nothing. I'll go in if you want me to, but I think we're safer down in the tunnels until the raid stops." His words were punctuated by another blast and the roof overhead fairly danced. Puffs of rubble drifted down around them. "It's possible Colin got out. There's not a whole lot left in there. Do you want me to go in?" Even as he talked, he reined in the crimson wave of rage that was Bogie. *An eye for an eye, a tooth for a tooth. . . .*

Amber's arms tightened and he had the distinct impression she'd squeezed her eyes shut. "No," she whispered finally. "I don't think he's in there."

He realized what she'd been trying to do. He knew she didn't like experimenting with the powers that could someday make her a killer, but he respected that she'd had enough courage to try. "But you're not sure."

"N-no. I . . . I just can't be sure. Please, let's go."

"All right then." He looked across the twisted lengths of tube and pipe that lay down spidery tracks inside the moon. "That way." He let Bogie's berserker spirit free. Jack let out a booming laugh as he and Bogie disintegrated the barriers between themselves and their destination.

"Jack! Jack!"

Amber's muffled voice broke his concentration. He eased his neck and shoulders under the burden of her body. "What is it?"

"Thank god."

He felt a dampness at the back of his neck. "I thought you'd never wake up," Amber said. She sniffed. "I've been yelling at you for ... well, forever."

"I didn't hear you."

"Didn't hear me? Dammit, I'm plastered to your back! How could you not hear me?"

But they both knew. Jack hadn't heard because Bogie had been overriding almost every sense he had. He lumbered to a stop and put the screws down on Bogie's protest and felt the other's mind shrink back in respect and fear.

He looked around. They were deep in the network of tunnels. Behind and overhead, the armor mikes filtered in the continuing sound of klaxons, punctuated by an explosion here and there. The strafing raid had turned into an all-out war. Governor Franken must have ordered the laser cannons to return fire. It was a small enough gesture, too little, too late. Hostilities had commenced. All the Thraks had to do was prove their aim accurate enough to blackmail Lasertown into surrendering. It wouldn't take much to remind Franken of Lasertown's precarious toe hold on this piece of rock, and norcite ore be damned.

Amber ducked her head dizzily as Jack moved. If she craned her head back far enough, she could get a semblance of the view that he commanded out of the face plate, but she wasn't sure she wanted to look. He'd done everything but walk through rock and that probably only because he hadn't considered it yet. They'd just

made a heart-stopping journey through bulkheads that closed even as they stepped through,
elevator shafts that were no longer operational
and had to be jumped, and rock walls that ava-
lanched as shock waves hit them.

Her heart still thumped in the backwash of
adrenalin from Bogie. She understood now why
Jack had not wished to replace the suit, treacherous though the destiny of the suit and its wearer
might be. It was worth the possible outcome to
be possessed like this, to walk life on an edge
ever sharp and exciting. She knew now that the
soul of the alien was a true warrior, lustful yet
calculating, and that, to a relatively gentle man
such as Jack, Bogie was as necessary as air and
water. Or, at least, she thought she understood
as she hid her eyes from the dizzying view of
destruction behind them.

"Quit moving for a while," Jack said impatiently.

"Would you like me to stop breathing, too?"

"It's an idea. The face plate keeps fogging.
One of us is doing far too much exhaling."

Amber sniffed sharply. Then her curiosity got
the better of her. "What are you doing?"

"Something I don't do much, even with this
equipment." He turned and faced a tunnel wall.
"There should be a parallel tunnel just a few
meters that way, unless I've lost my bearings. I
want to take some soundings to make sure."

Amber groaned. *Now* he was thinking of going
through solid rock. She felt Jack sigh. "All right,
all right. I'll hold my breath or whatever."

"Just hold still. I don't want to miss the readings."

She closed her eyes and laid her cheek against the back of his neck as he did his work. It seemed a complicated procedure and his sweat trickled down and puddled across her cheekbone as he paced, knelt, drilled a core, stepped back and did a few more things.

Then, he muttered. "Hold on *now*."

She felt nothing different, but in a matter of seconds, she could feel the excitement running through his bones. "That's it!"

"You got it?"

"Yes."

"Now what are you going to try to do?"

"Find my crew."

"What makes you think they're down here?"

"Because, right now, it's the safest place to be. I can't contact them because our coms aren't on the same frequency. If I had enough room in here, I could make the adjustment, but—"

"I know, blame it on me," Amber said.

"Did I mention any names?"

In spite of herself, she grinned. Once, she had wondered if she would ever banter with Jack again. Impulsively, she hugged him tighter. He made a choking noise. She let go. "What if they are there? That's rock between us."

"Not exactly. It's pocketed throughout this section. And, if I'm lucky, I might hit one of the membranes."

"Membranes?" She didn't understand what he was talking about. Jack explained briefly about the tunnels with membranes which could be penetrated briefly and self-sealed. It was possible to get into a tunnel without damaging its integrity.

"Meaning, if it still had air, I could get out of this suit?"

"Something like that."

"Well, then," and Amber giggled, "I'm right behind you."

He took a deep breath and prepared to put a fair-sized hole in the tunnel section. This tube was not pressurized, but he couldn't guarantee that the roof might not cave in on him. He felt Amber take a breath also. Then she made a noise of surprise.

"Listen."

He did, but the mikes weren't transmitting anything. "I don't hear it."

"That's it! When did the shock waves stop?"

"I don't know." Too embarrassed to admit he'd heard very little while Bogie rode herd over him, he said nothing else. He listened a moment, then added, "I think the bombings are over. They'll be in as soon as possible to dig us out and to assess the damage."

Some of which you're responsible for, Amber thought but did not say. Cut off as they had been, there'd been no other way. She squeezed her eyes shut as he said, "Hold on, we're going through."

It wasn't just the laser blast or the gauntlets tearing aside chunks of red-hot rock, or the swaggering gait of the suit in a power walk—it was the wash of sheer rage from Bogie that staggered her mind, forcing her chin up and eyes open despite her best intentions as Jack took them through. She saw the opalescent, shimmering membrane emerge across a pocket in rock, a web reflecting the suit's color back at her. They came to a halt directly in front of it.

"We're going through that?" Her chin jabbed Jack in the back of his shoulder and he complained, then said, "Carefully."

"We'll rip it."

"Might. The membranes are used mainly with waldos. They'll allow a very slow penetration and self-seal around it."

"Meaning they will seal behind us after we've gone through?"

"In theory. If I do it right. Be glad we haven't hit a vein of norcite yet. It's got an extremely high melting point."

Amber held tight, feeling Jack's heat on her flesh, even through her suit and overrobe, felt him burn like a fire banked deep inside.

He muttered, "Don't move now. I don't want the holo to catch something you've done and step it up, all right?"

Her shoulders and the small of her back ached from clinging to him. Various gadgets at the back of the suit dug into her skin, making pock marks and bruises she was sure would never go away. If they survived this, she reminded herself. She whispered, "I'm ready."

With a grace that denied gravity and minute movements that contradicted the sheer power of the battle armor, Jack extended his hand and began to penetrate the membrane as though he were a delicate instrument instead of a walking war machine.

The web wavered. It stretched to its utmost limit, then, gently, began to swallow the gauntlet. When it had allowed the suit penetration nearly to the shoulder, Jack rocked back slightly to shift his balance and stepped forward. She felt the strain as Bogie fought Jack's control and she took her wonder away from what they were doing to focus on the alien's emotions. She took the brunt of it full force. Her ears rang as his psychic shouts roared through her. Mirroring Jack's movement through the membrane, she delicately pushed through Bogie's rage until she absorbed it ... for the moment. The cords on her neck strained. She felt the parallel tension in Jack as he stepped forward and, finally, was able to put his foot down.

Then, like sliding into a pond of wild water, something Amber had never seen on Malthen, but had seen videos of, they were through.

Jack sucked in his breath sharply as he surveyed the rear cameras and then exhaled. "We've done it."

"Which means?"

"There should be air on the other side of this bulkhead." He tapped the controls. It opened, letting them into the tunnel. The auxiliary light system was on here, lending the area a half-glow.

It was empty. Jack sealed the bulkhead behind them and surveyed the section. It was older and if he remembered correctly, beyond the far bulkhead was another section leading to one of the supply elevator shafts. He lumbered to a stop and checked the suit gauges.

At this rate, with the two of them sharing the suit, the air would last perhaps another twenty-six hours. Not bad, except that the damage to the mine had been such that it would probably be at least that long before they could be pulled out. Weighing possibilities, he unscrewed the helmet.

Amber gulped, then said, "Bleah."

"What's wrong?"

"The air in here is better than the air out there. With the possible exception of how much more you're going to sweat."

He bent a little and began to open a seam. Bogie had gone, suddenly, completely, and left Jack with a hollowed out feeling, as though he'd given all he could give and had nothing left. He took a deep breath as the armor opened up. Amber clung to him. He swung his shoulders. "Come on, get out."

"Is it safe?"

"For now."

She slid to the ground. Her legs buckled under her and she collapsed in a heap. Jack, half-peeled out of the suit, bent down. "Are you all right?"

"Oh, fine. Never been better. Now I know what a sandwich in shrink wrap feels like." Amber sucked in her cheeks in parody and then laughed. She pushed her tangled mane of honey blonde hair back from a face that, although too thin, hit him like a load of norcite ore. He straightened back up abruptly.

Just how long had he been chilled down? How much time had she had to grow up?

"What'll we do now?"

"Wait." Somewhat awkwardly, he made the suit sit down. She looked at him.

"Aren't you getting out?"

"No. I don't think so."

Her large eyes blinked thoughtfully and then she asked, "Why?"

"This is old tunnel. It could spring a leak just from the strain. Besides, I don't know if they're done with up there or not. I can get you back in if something happens, but not both of us. So I'll just be uncomfortable a little while longer, okay?"

"Okay." Amber swallowed, her face a little paler than it had been. She slipped a hand over his gauntlet, then said, "D'you think I could hold your real hand for a while?"

"Sure." He pulled his arm out and laced her fingers into his. She was a little cool. "It's not over yet."

"I guess not," she murmured, leaning against him. Quite suddenly, she fell asleep.

Jack felt the snap of Bogie as soon as her eyes shut and he knew why she was so exhausted. But Bogie seemed drained, too. *Fight more, boss?*

"No. Not for a while."

Okay. Rest is good, too.

He felt the alien presence withdraw.

"Rest is very good," Jack echoed. He leaned back against the tunnel and closed his eyes wearily. They had a wait ahead of them, anyhow. He felt a moment's keen disappointment that no

one else had made it this far. After a rest, he'd
adjust the com frequency and see what he could
pick up. He wouldn't sleep long, he never did.
Just in case he couldn't wake up one of these
times.

Jack woke abruptly, with a strangling feeling,
and gulped for air, his head throbbing with a
dull but massive headache. He had dreamed of
a massive saurian being, reaching out to grasp
him and pull him up, up from the vast deepness
of a stagnant lake. He looked out, unseeing, forcing his eyes wide but not really registering where
he was. Amber lay against him like a dead
weight.

He tried to swallow, his tongue thick and
swollen. What was wrong here? What had he
been dreaming? He took his hand away from
hers and scrubbed at his face. God, but he
couldn't think. His head pounded and pounded—

Abruptly, Jack reached for his helmet and
pulled it on. He scanned his readouts. Shit! The
air was going bad rapidly. This unit might be
sealed, but the recyclers had shut down. He had
to suit up and fast.

"Amber! Wake up! C'mon. There's no time to
waste."

"Mugh," she said and her head lolled around
loosely on her shoulders. He shook her.

"Wake up!"

Bleared eyes came open. "Jack?" and then she
gave a sweet smile. "I love you, Jack."

"Right. Now wake up!" He pulled her into the
suit. She flopped against him and he sealed the

armor, even though she wasn't even near being in position.

He gasped at the sudden intimacy of their bodies, caught his breath and re-seated the helmet, then set the air controls. Amber happily sighed and wrapped her arms around his bare waist, snuggling her nose against his chest. Jack swallowed tightly and stood straight up, as if by holding his breath he could pull away from the disturbing closeness of her body. The suit's air filtered in and he could feel the loosening of the steel band of a headache that had been threatening to take the top of his head off.

Amber revived slowly. She looked up, wedged in just under his chin. "Jack? What are you doing?"

"The air was bad out there."

"But I'm not in position. We can't possibly do anything like this." Then, mischievously, she added, "Well, we can do one thing I can think of like this, but this is hardly the time or place." Her embrace tightened intimately.

Jack could have sworn the quarters were too tight for it, but he jumped.

Amber laughed. "Why, Jack! You're shy!"

"Amber!"

"All right, all right." Laboriously, she began to sidle around him. "Can't you open up for just a second? I don't think I can get up on your back . . . no, wait a minute . . ." Her hands grabbed the back of his shoulders and tightened. "Let me see. . . there!"

Jack let out a low, quavering sigh of relief.

She tickled his ear before wrapping her arms loosely around his neck.

The air revived her to the point where she suddenly realized the seriousness of their situation. "How long were we under?"

"Almost twelve hours, believe it or not. We're lucky I woke up." Luck? He'd dreamed . . . no. No, the dream hadn't woke him. Or had it?

"What are we going to do?"

"We're going to have to get out and get out now. This section's no good. I won't hurt anything by blasting through the seals."

"Jack. You can't blast your way to the surface."

He paused before the bulkhead, his gauntlet cocked, but his fingertips not at the control patch yet. "Why not?"

"We can't—you can't possibly—this must be solid rock."

He smiled, though she couldn't see it. "That's the beauty of it, Amber. This part of the mining operation isn't solid rock. It's pocketed all the way through. That's why we had to put in tube sections for the tunnels. Only way to keep the tunnels pressurized and airtight. And if we're lucky . . . we'll hit a lot of pockets on the way up."

"If you know which way is up. Suppose we get stuck trying to tunnel our way through and out the other side. How much of a charge do you carry?"

She'd made a point. The armor didn't carry enough of a charge to blast continuously through. Or enough air. And there were other considerations as well. He could ignore the hunger pains beginning to cramp his lean stomach, but the nagging fullness of his bladder was another matter. And, there was Amber. He didn't know how long he could continue to carry her about the way he'd been doing. But he could blast through to the elevator shaft. The suit had enough hover power, maybe, to lift both of them up and out.

Unless he'd miscalculated on how many levels down they'd gone.

Jack mentally shook off that thought. They were dead, anyway, if they stayed down here.

"Don't say that," Amber whispered huskily at his ear. "I don't want to hear it."

He hadn't realized he'd voiced his last thought aloud. He swiveled his head and squeezed one of her hands between his chin and his shoulder momentarily, a gesture meant to comfort her. "That'll never happen."

"Good. I was hoping you weren't giving up. What about the com lines?"

Again, he couldn't pull his arm back and out of a sleeve to adjust the frequency scanner, they were wedged in so tightly. He felt Amber wiggle.

"Is that it?"

A hand pointed just under his chin.

"Yes."

She moved with sudden intensity and reached forward. Breathlessly, Amber said, "I can just reach it. What'll I do?"

"Touch the blue square. That's all. And it'll home in by itself once it scans a working frequency." Jack tried to ignore the urgent pressing of young, ripe feminine physique against his bare back as she stretched.

"Got it!"

They both sighed as Amber settled back into place. Jack listened to dead air for a few moments, then re-aimed his gauntlet and fired at the bulkhead in front of him.

The tunnel, as they climbed through and into it, had been cracked like an egg—and around it sat, like shards of its shell, the crew, gray suits settled in apathetic lumps about the area.

"Jack!"

"I see them."

"Are they—dead?"

He didn't know. He walked over to the nearest heap and nudged it. The man fell over rigidly and he could see through the face plate that the miner was dead, suffocated. "Damn it."

"Is he—"

"Yes. But he wouldn't be if they'd kept the suits fully charged." Anger boiled in him at the uselessness of it. Bogie awoke suddenly.

Kill them for you, boss.

"We've got to get back, first." He straightened and went to the next suit. Perez' name was stenciled across the shoulder. Jack swallowed tightly and reached out to the suit.

The man sat up and grabbed his hand at the touch just as the armor's com lines tingled into life.

"Man! Where'd you come from?"

Jack pointed to the blasted bulkhead and Perez let out a slow whistle. The digger began excitedly to rouse his comrades. One or two had suffocated in their sleep, like the first, but the rest got shakily to their feet. Amber let out a squeal of joy as she recognized St. Colin's well-made, well-aged face looking up at them.

"Well, well," he said. "An angel of mercy come to deliver us."

Stash walked from the far end of the tunnel. "Don't be too sure, mate. 'e seems to be in the same mess we are."

Jack eyed the New Aussie. "Don't be too sure. Where's Boggs?"

A grunt, breaking up over the com, and then, "Don't know. He might not have made it out."

Perez added, "We got separated, man. Blasts going off everywhere. The Bugs have done us in this time."

"What have you been doing?"

"Downtime." Colin spoke up, suddenly. "We're all low on air, as you can see. Amber, I can hear you, but I can't see you."

"I'm in here with Jack."

A low chuckle. "I see. That must be close quarters."

Jack grinned in spite of himself. "You don't know the half of it. Stash—what's on the other side of the bulkhead?"

"Th' elevator, o' course. But it's filled with a rock slide."

"Filled?"

The deepsuit containing Stash shrugged. "We took a look as soon as the dust settled. It came in on our heels."

"How far up?"

Stash eyed him sardonically. "Thinking of digging out?"

"That's the idea."

"Never make it. You'd have to blast your way through at least one, maybe two levels. And then, the machinery's down. You have an open shaft above you. How are you going to get through that?"

"If you'd finished Basic, you'd know." Jack turned from Stash back to Perez. "Start emergency broadcast. We've been down here long enough that somebody's started a rescue search. You're too low on air not to risk the power drain."

Protests filtered in over the line. Perez put his gloves up. "C'mon, diggers—you all know it's true. We might as well yell as long as we've got breath left."

Stash made an ironic bow as Jack approached the ineffectively sealed bulkhead.

Jack took a stance, aimed and blew the end of the tunnel away. When the air cleared, he stood up to his knees in fine, gray dust.

Over the com, someone murmured, "Shee-it."

But ahead of Jack was a tumble of rock and it reached up the shaft as far as he could see—which wasn't far. His gaze flicked back to his gauges. Not red field—yet. But as the solar panels weren't even getting a rudimentary charge, he knew after all the blasting he'd done to get this far, he was running low. And the suit was using energy twice as fast to maintain the two of them.

Amber squeezed his neck, sensing his hesitation. "Go for it."

He waded into the silt as far as he could go, rear cameras reflecting the crew at his back moving farther away, out of range of the slide. "Hold on," he said to Amber. "We could get buried in this stuff."

"Buried one way or another," she answered lightly. "What's the difference?"

"Right. Let Bogie go."

"What? Oh." And she said nothing further that could be mistaken over the com lines.

But his mind flooded with the strength and the fury of the berserker. Be damned if Jack was going to be buried quietly at the bottom of an elevator shaft! Be damned if life was going to end here, quietly, whimpering!

He blasted away and hit the power vault as rock powdered away before and around him. He hit his gauntlets full on, for rock splinters and shrapnel could do as much damage as a projectile weapon. Now he dusted it down before him, in a running river of fine motes that bathed the suit in an angry red-orange glow as they cooled. Over the com lines, he could hear the shouts and scrambles of diggers working to channel the fall away from them as he rose in the shaft, blasting his way out.

The suit strained. He could hear the whine and groan as the hover protested the overload. He rose, not smoothly, but in a herky-jerky movement that rattled the whole armor. Jack looked up and saw the ceiling, a jumble of boulders, abruptly give way and he shot out a spray of fire that turned it into a molten waterfall.

"Holy shit," someone cried below him as he cleared the first level.

Ironically, St. Colin said, "I'll second that, young man."

Perez' accented voice excitedly broadcast, "Use the segment there to channel it that way, man, or we're buried. Hurry up, move it, move it!"

The sense of it was crimson-curtained away from him by Bogie's intensity. Jack's chest swelled as he fought upward. Another level. And then, falteringly, another.

Amber clung tightly. She quivered as the suit did. "Jack," she whispered. "What does that film of red over the gauges mean?"

"Nothing." He aimed, this time carefully, trying to angle the blast to do the most good, for it might be the last he would make. The hover fought to maintain their height, not meant to climb endlessly into the air.

The rock broke away, as intended, and, as not intended but fortunate, left a ledge to the side of the shaft. He fired a side thrust, and maneuvered them over to the ledge and let the suit settle. The hover cut off almost gratefully.

He took a deep breath. "I've gone as far as I can."

The cameras scanned upward. It wasn't far enough. Another two or three levels stretched above them, clear, but inaccessible.

"Oh, Jack." Amber bent her face and he could feel the moisture from her eyes mingling with the salt of his own sweat.

"Say again, miner one, we hear you. Please repeat so that we can get a fix on you. This is Rescue Operations."

Jack jumped. "I'm down here, Rescue. One of

the supply elevators. Another four levels below me, we've got a tunnel full of what's left of Crew Two."

"Keep talking, miner one. We'll drop a line as soon as we get the doors open."

Jack heard the muffled blast above and the shaft shivered. He watched on his screen as the silvery hoist rope snaked down to them.

"I've nearly got it. Lower, lower, there—that's it!" He reached out and grabbed the lifeline.

"Okay, miner one. I'm gonna tell you how to make a rappel sling, so we can haul you up."

Jack already had the line fixed about him. "We're already ready. Haul away." He tilted his head back and looked upward, to where the cracked doors let through the harsh white light of unfiltered starshine. The suit rose hesitantly into the air, and then smoothly, swiftly, up the elevator shaft.

Hands reached for him, helped him out of the sling, voices talking all at once, as he untied the line.

"How many down there?"

"Shift Two Crew, about twenty-five."

"And St. Colin of the Blue Wheel," Amber blurted out.

"Ah." A tall, imposing figure came to the fore and as he leaned forward, the face of their rescuer came toward the front of the face plate, visible for the first time. "The good Walker will be in diplomatic custody, for the time being. The rest of you will be held in the barracks once temps are set up."

Jack's blood ran cold. He looked into the visage of a full-blooded Thrakian commander.

CHAPTER 16

"Well, I don't bloody like it," Stash said, kicking at a bunk. "Tradin' one master for another. Even if we are beddin' down in the exec quarters."

Boggs sat wearily on a far bed, hunched over, his hands cradling his face. He'd spent most of the night identifying bodies brought up from operations, as Bull Quade was dead and the shift supervisor for Crew One was still missing. "Shut up, Stash," he said. "We don't know what they want. We're prisoners of war right now."

"Course you know what they want from us," the New Aussie pressed. He ran a hand through his butcher-cut black hair and scowled. "They want us to keep bringin' out the norcite for them."

Jack was working on his armor in the corner, only half-listening to the others talk as he wondered how Amber was doing. St. Colin had persuaded the Thrakian field commander to take her in under diplomatic custody also and she'd gone with the Walker back to the hotel under martial guard. Most of the crew were still asleep, unsettled in the exec quarters, unused to these more comfortable surroundings, and wary of their captors. He chiseled off a last flake of molten rock, now cooled, and buffed down the Flexalinks. Operations would see to its charging. He didn't intend to go down in the mines without his armor again.

"I don't want any bloody Bug telling me when I can eat and sleep and sh—"

"That's enough," Boggs interrupted. "What are you going to do about it? The nearest Dominion troop dispatch is three months away."

Stash stopped and smiled darkly. "Wot can we do about it, you ask, mate? Well, I'll tell you. There's more of us than them. And this time, if we try anything, the whole bloody town will be on our side. We'll be heroes! I don't know if your 'ead was swivelin' around when they marched us in here, but I was lookin'! And those bloody laser cannons are situated, just like these offices, outside the domes. Won't take much to get to 'em.''

Jack had seen the cannons, too. "They're not only outside the domes, Stash, they're outside the mining base, too. Any man going out has no protection whatsoever. He's only as good as his deepsuit."

The other shrugged. "There's a little risk."

"There's a lot of risk. Do you think those Thraks are going to leave the cannons operational? They're probably working on them right now."

"Yeah, but it'll take three, four days to do the job right." Stash met Jack's eyes as he crossed the room. "We could put it right if we don't waste any more time. Man as handy as you shouldn't be too worried about doin' it."

Jack put away the last of his tools and stood up. He'd been thinking along similar lines and dismissed it. If only Amber wasn't being held.... "I'm not worried about it, Stash. I'm going to get in that soft bed and put in some downtime, because the new foreman's going to be here in the morning and I can guarantee you, we're going to be putting in a lot of time in the tunnels. They're going to strip as much norcite as they can out of here—hit and run, before the Dominion catches up with them. We can either be an asset or a liability. Do you want to talk about what Thraks do to liabilities?"

Stash tried to stare him down, but it was the new Aussie who gave way, blinking and then ducking his head. "Right, mate," he mumbled finally. "But you think about it."

"I'll be thinking about a lot of things," Jack answered. He picked the bed closest to Bogie and lay down, drawing the thin blanket over him and turning his back to the rest of the room. Crew One was isolated in another part of the exec building and he wondered why. He was also wondering why the Thraks had taken such a risk with Lasertown when there were other norcite operations to go after. Unless the norcite wasn't the only attraction here. Franken had been clandestinely digging at the archaeological site, the Walkers were foaming at the mouth to get out there—and from the Thrakian interest in Crew One, which had been working there off and on, Jack's best guess was that the site was of keen interest to them, too. But why?

The last thought that crossed Jack's mind before he slept was of Fritzi. Nothing had been found of the big man. Had he gone into narcosis and wandered off to his death or been caught by strafing fire? He would contact Gail as soon as he could. He owed Fritzi that much.

He woke fitfully a few hours later. The red glow of the sentry's night light bathed the room. He could hear the rhythmic breathing and snores of his fellows. Jack looked over wonderingly, for his battle armor stood next to the bed, gauntlet out a little, curved over his head like a protective shield. He stared up at the suit and knew he did not remember the bed having been this close to the armor.

He should be scared of it, he knew, for it had the potential of consuming him and the more he wore it, the closer he came to that destiny. But the voice and strength that had buoyed him these last few days seemed to be more, to promise more. Funny, he'd meant to discuss that with Amber. Did the berserker contain the germ of being more than a killing beast? Could it have thoughts, and even a soul, beyond that?

The hair rose on the back of his neck in tiny prickles. Jack cleared his throat and lay back down. He was very, very close to the edge, he thought, if he was beginning to consider Bogie to be friendly. As soon as he got back, he'd get himself measured for a new suit. The secrets of this one he was afraid to learn.

As he closed his eyes, he thought he heard a whisper:

Jack.

He ignored it.

Amber stared in fascination at the Thrakian commander as the being stood, courteously and gracefully, listening to Colin's persuasion. She'd heard Jack describe them before, but she'd never seen one in her life, not in the flesh. Or in the chitin, which seemed more applicable. An insect of sorts, equally at home balanced back on two legs or sloping forward on four, somewhat armored, and with a sharp-planed head or face that was almost faceted like a gemstone. But, unlike an insect, this creature was fleshy and dexterous. It was capable of speaking and it breathed the air of the Lasertown domes without trouble, except that it carried a small tube with it through which it inhaled from time to time, as though augmenting the air mix or perhaps dousing the smell of the humans it had coraled. It was definitely a he. Though uninformed, she had no doubt of its gender.

"My dear Talthos. If we're merely under house arrest for our protection and your main interest is the mines, surely we can come to some sort of agreement for my aides to investigate the archaeological site. We'll be no trouble. We require no manpower and I will allow you to place a guard over us for security, if you wish." Colin smiled. "I can guarantee you that we're not going to launch a counterattack from there."

"No," breathed the Thraks. It was his sixth

"no" in as many attempts. He obviously did not believe in arguing.

"No to the dig or to the guard? I'm willing to negotiate, but you must give me something to begin with."

"No," said the Thraks. His chest chitin expanded. "We do not believe it is in your best interest to conduct a dig at the site, your saintedness."

Amber hid a yawn. This predawn meeting had awakened her from a very restless night. She looked out the hotel window at the gray-filmed dome. She was not normally a morning person anyway, but out there, who could tell? Seasons could come and go with a sameness that was indistinguishable. It was as though time had stopped in Lasertown. She felt inexplicably melancholy.

Colin stopped. He scratched his head, ruffling the thinning hair behind his right ear. "Commander, my men are expert deepsuit users as well as diggers. Our excavation will not place additional demands on your rule here, I promise that. If you could just let me demonstrate. It's most important that this site be investigated before any retaliation from the Triad throne destroys the area."

Amber braced herself for another no, but the Thraks straightened. "Maybe," he answered.

Colin almost missed it. Then he brightened. "A demonstration, commander? When?"

"Tomorrow."

"Ah. Good."

"I will forward details to you later. My presence is required elsewhere. Good . . . day," and Talthos bowed himself out.

As the door schussed closed after him, Colin slapped his hands together. "Well. That's something."

"Crumbs," Amber muttered.

"Perhaps. Perhaps it's just another delaying tactic. What do you think?"

"I think," Amber said, as she uncurled from the couch and stood up, "that I'm terribly hungry."

The Walker laughed. "That much I can definitely obtain for you. Find out if Lenska is awake and we'll go get breakfast."

Boggs mopped up the last of his hash and said, around the mouthful, "Well, Stash, at least the chow around here has improved."

"Not enough, mate." Stash sat back.

Jack watched, thinking that Stash was the sort of man who would never be content. With anything.

"What do you mean, not enough?"

"If they want me to work for them, they're going to have to provide certain amenities."

Jack smiled. "And here I thought you'd be offering to provide them with the amenities."

The crew sitting at that table laughed and Stash scowled. His black winged eyebrow frowned downward. "You know what I mean, mate."

"Of course I do. We all do. My advice to you is that you keep your mouth shut and do a lot of listening over the next few shifts. We don't really know what the Thraks want with us or what they intend to do to us. A little caution will go a long way."

Boggs threw down his disposable napkin. "I suggest you listen, Stash. We've got the new foreman coming down this morning to talk to us before he breaks us up into work parties. If the norcite is so damned valuable to them, why'd they damage the mines so heavily? We might be a hell of a lot more expendable than you think."

Outnumbered, Stash shrugged and glared at Jack. "I kept my mouth shut about you bein' a bloody Knight, didn't I? I know how to gamble." And he sat, sullen, without another word while the table was policed around him, and the crew gathered to wait for the new foreman.

Jack shook his head as Boggs held out a pack of stim gum and watched as the older man stuffed a wad between his gum and his cheek. His bald head shone in the artificial lighting of the mess hall, revealing bristling hairs stuck randomly here and there. The hairs in his ears wiggled as he began to chew vigorously. What would it be like to grow old as a contract laborer and need a cheek full of stim to get the aches and pains out in the morning so you could keep up on the job?

He looked away as an odor wafted down the corridor and his hands grew cold. He knew that smell. Jack was halfway to his feet when the doors opened, and the impressive figure of the new foreman pushed his way in.

Perez' jaw fell open. "Jeezus," he muttered and his dark skin lightened a little.

The foreman halted, something shadowy and

even bigger waiting in his wake beyond the door. Jack's mouth dried out suddenly.

"I be Captain K'rok. I be a Milot, a valiant and valued soldier who was saved from his planet's conquering by the Thraks. I fought long and hard and earned their respect. Now I be in command of you," and the Milot bared his canines as he gave them all a hard grin.

Tall and broad, shaggy with a dense, two-coat fur that had oils similar to those of sheep, the bear-headed humanoid looked them over. His dark hide had grizzled, showing his age, and Jack knew, as he sat and looked at the being, that he was watching one of his nightmares come to life. It was true that the Thraks, occasionally, adopted a defeated foe as one of their own if that foe had impressed them. For a Milot, Jack knew, it meant that this one had undoubtedly been one of the meanest and trickiest, for the Milots were a truly treacherous bunch. He wondered how short a leash the Thraks had K'rok on to keep him in line.

As if sensing hostile thoughts, K'rok stood aside slightly to let whatever it was following him shoulder into the mess hall doorway. "Lest you think I be a target or not to be obeyed, this be my bodyguard."

The saurian monstrosity edged partially into the hall, the brilliant frill around its neck down, but its claws out.

Jack tried to swallow and couldn't. Boggs opened his mouth, unaware of the wad of gum and spittle that fell to the table with a damp plop.

"Good god a-mighty, what is *that?*"

The Milot swung a glance Boggs' way and grinned broadly. "This be a berserker, human. Legendary warrior lizard from my home planet. Mean son of a bitch."

Jack felt a tremor in his limbs he could not control.

With relish the Milot added, "It grows from eggs it lays in dead flesh. Sometimes live flesh. Human flesh feeds eggs real good. One of you be disobedient, perhaps I let my berserker plant eggs. I can always use another good berserker."

In the far corner, someone lost his breakfast. The pungent smell mingled unpleasantly with the rank odor of the Milot and his bodyguard.

The Milot's grin never wavered. "Now let me tell you what I and Commander Talthos expects of you."

Jack hardly heard. He forced every muscle to stop its twitching, palsied dance. He placed his hands on his thighs and gripped tightly, trying with every breath to still the terror that had leaped full-blown into his system and fought to panic every brain cell he had right out of his skull. But he could not escape it. *That*, that was what he could become if he continued to let Bogie live!

CHAPTER 17

Jack told the others that he had to hide the battle armor away from the Milot, who would undoubtedly recognize it as the weapon it could be, and they all accepted that explanation for his not wearing it. Stash particularly seemed to interpret the gesture as an indication that Jack had joined the private rebellion being planned against the Thrakian rule. Talthos, not a veteran of the Sand Wars, hadn't known the suit when he'd seen it but K'rok was bound to—if only because his berserker had undoubtedly sprung from the incubating shelter of one such suit.

He worked three full days of double-shifts before K'rok let him get a com through to Amber, but all in all, the Milot was a fair enough master. He had a directive to get the mines clear enough to work and he had sense enough to know that the crew needed the freedom to do what had to be done and the incentive to do it quickly. The incentive was a ticket out of Lasertown the minute the Thraks decided to pull out.

The persuasion was a little more subtle. K'rok had a habit of letting small, furry mammals lose in the tunnels for the berserker to chase down and consume. Typically saurian, the beast ate relatively little but even one such meal impressed the whole shift working at the time.

Boggs had shuddered, but Stash became philosophical. "Reminds me, mates, of a fellow I worked for once. Had a great big aquarium he did, with a great big, nasty fish in it. Used to feed it little fish which it would eat up all squirming and tearing like. Made his point, he did."

Freshly showered and exhausted, Jack sat down in front of the visiphone, one of the perks of occupying the exec offices. The com line buzzed and then Amber came on.

"Jack! What's happening? Are you all right? You look pale."

"I'm fine. They're working us hard, that's all. But fair. Food rations are better and the contracts will be terminated when they pull out."

She made a face. "And I thought we had you out of there."

He shrugged. "Better than what happened to the governor."

"I know. I heard about that. Fried her at her post, although there are some whispers around that she did it to herself." Amber's eyes were very wide and round with the implication of the gossip.

Jack smiled in spite of himself. "How's St. Colin?"

"Fit to be tied. The Thraks won't budge about the digging. He's . . ." and Jack lost most of the sense of what she said, then her image cleared and Amber's lightly freckled nose was wrinkled in dismay. "Censored," she added.

Jack understood. The com line was tapped. The transmission was being jammed when it was considered necessary. "You just be a good girl," he said. "The Thraks are treating us honorably."

"Right. So how's Bogie?"

"Who?" Jack said blandly.

"Bogie," she repeated. "Jack—"

"Not now," he interrupted. "I've been working double-shifts and I've got to take whatever downtime I can get."

She blinked, then comprehension that he didn't wish to discuss the suit with her dawned. She nodded. "Okay. Well, you sleep tight then, okay?"

"That I will. K'rok may be a Milot, but he is a good commander. Remember that." He signed off with a faint echo of Amber saying, "... a Milot," reaching him before the connection ended. He had no doubt she'd put that together. She had the street savvy that would protect her. Now all he had to do was protect himself.

He returned to the sleeping quarters and went in quietly, the room's hush broken by snoring already begun. The snap of playing cards was gone, even Boggs and Stash dead asleep in hard-worked exhaustion. He went to his bunk and sat down.

Underneath, his armor lay quietly. Jack's bare ankle brushed the Flexalinks and almost instantaneously, Bogie's sentience sprang into life.

Wear me now, boss?

225

"No," Jack returned. He found it hard to swallow. He jerked his foot away, but the mind-touch followed.

Free. We'll fight free.

"No."

I'll keep you safe.

"No." Jack withdrew onto his bunk and pulled his cover up tightly, burying himself.

Wear me, Boss. We must go—

"Go?" Jack rubbed his head. He couldn't force Bogie into silence and out of his head. And the suit wanted most desperately to go somewhere. Go where?

Calling. . . .

Jack took a deep breath and got hold of himself. Closing his eyes, he began a series of mental commands that he hadn't used in months, lapsing into the mental discipline of becoming, being a Knight. Bogie's hold faded and then slipped away altogether.

He slept. But at the edge of his consciousness, a something nibbled, a call that begged to be answered.

"They lost another man on Crew One last night," Perez said conspiratorially.

"Runaway?"

"No. No, man, they said the sleeping sickness got him. They say," and he lowered his voice even more, his slender hand gripping the breakfast table, "they say they lost a lot of them when the domes were under fire. People trying to get out all over the place." Bailey and Ron gave him a dirty look and returned to their meals.

Jack looked at the laborer. "Perez, anybody will panic when they're being shot at."

"No, man. They say—"

"I be saying Crew Two is late this morning." K'rok's huge and smelly shadow drifted over them.

"Yes, sir." They scrambled off the chairs and out to the staging area, the temporary shop set up for suiting.

Jack brushed past the Milot, trying to avoid looking at the slavering berserker towering behind him. K'rok held one of his feeder mammals in one hand, absently stroking it preparatory to releasing it, and the bodyguard was working itself into a feeding frenzy at the sight of a meal before it.

Jack turned his face away, knowing that the little creature would shortly be scraps of fur and bone.

The Milot sensed Jack's repulsion. He let out a bark of Milosian laughter. "You have a healthy respect for my berserker, eh, Storm?"

"You might say that."

The Milot dogged Jack's steps to the shop. "Why be that? I have heard you were a hero and saved most of Crew One. That is some tale I heard."

"Embellished," Jack said. He reached for the rack and his deepsuit. "What about you? What did you do to impress the Thraks?"

"Ah. You be knowing about the Sand Wars? You too young for that. You would be just a pup."

"My father went down at Dorman's Stand."

"Ah. I fought long and hard for Milos."

"How do you feel being one of the last?" Jack asked. His voice had gone hard, but K'rok didn't seem to notice, unused to the subleties of human behavior.

K'rok shrugged. "There be some of us. My mate is a good breeder. We will begin again. Not like berserkers here. They—how do you say it—regenerate. All one needs is a tiny scrap of hide."

"I thought they laid eggs."

"Sometimes. Sometimes it is necessary to kill all berserkers off. Kill or be killed, eh?"

Jack blinked. His hand trembled a little as he opened the suit up to put on. A scrap of hide. Regeneration. He thought of the chamois at his back—the chamois that many of his fellow Knights had affected as well on Milos. Regeneration into a parasitic embryo that—

Boggs, paling a little, shoved past Jack and blocked the Milot as he eyed the small fuzzy. "You're not going to let that go in here."

"No, no, human. Maybe not. Maybe I drop it down the front of one of your suits and let my berserker go after it there, huh?" K'rok stalked away, booming with laughter and the berserker slavered after him.

Boggs turned and bellowed at Jack, "Get the slag out! One man late on shift makes us all late."

Jack turned unseeing eyes the shift boss' way, then shook himself like a drowning man coming out of the water. Boggs grumbled and turned away to his own suit. He didn't like K'rok menacing his men. He wasn't sure what the Milot had said to Jack, but the man was not one to be easily rocked. He didn't like what he'd just seen.

St. Colin walked into the room, his shoulders hunched over with fatigue, and, with a sigh that rattled harshly, dropped down on a chair. Amber came over and perched behind him and began lightly kneading the Walker's bowed shoulders. He was showing his age suddenly, shockingly, and she worried. The religious leader had found a place in her heart next to Jack's and she found herself wondering what she would do when it was time for them to go their separate ways.

He reached up and patted her hand. "You know what comforts me, girl."

She leaned down. "Jack always liked me to rub his neck, too."

"Heard from him yet today?"

"No. He's probably double-shifted again."

"Mmmm." Colin shrugged out of his brilliant blue robe. He eased the neckline of his simple jumpsuit. "The miners are thinning out quickly, from what I've been able to gather. This last group of laborers was recruited aggressively—"

"No kidding," Amber interrupted as she kneaded out a tightly bunched muscle.

"Well, that aside, they'd just released a shipload of laborers who'd worked out their contracts and were short of hands. Plus, there've been a lot of fatalities on Crew One."

"What kind of fatalities?"

"More than the usual mining accidents. Amber," and Colin turned around, displacing her hands, so he could look her in the eye. "Have you heard anything unusual? Gossip, that sort of thing?"

"Me?"

He stared patiently and she pinked. "Well, I guess I do have a way of finding things out."

"What have you heard?"

"Nothing much. There's something going on most people won't talk about—a kind of psychosis, from what I can gather. People just go walking out of the domes."

"Hysterical suicide?"

"I don't know if it's hysterical or not—but going for a walk outside the domes without a deepsuit is definitely suicide. And the ones that want to take the walk are real determined to do it."

"And it's worse in Crew One and other people who've been at the site."

Amber got down off her perch and sat on the level chair next to him. "It is?"

'From what I can gather, yes. That might explain why the Thraks won't let us go out, keep toying with us, and why Franken, rest her soul, put us off for months."

She put a hand on his knee and felt the intense level of his fatigue and worry. It frightened her. "What do you think it is?"

"God only knows. But it makes it even more imperative to get out there. I must see it. I must know what's going on."

"Hey! Don't you start thinking about taking a walk."

Colin laughed. "No, my dear, don't worry about

me. I may be obsessed, but I am not yet compulsed. But I want you to know and understand that I may have to take steps which Talthos won't like. I won't leave Lasertown without having seen the dig. And I have contacted an accomplice within Crew Two who might be able to make a big enough distraction to grant my wishes."

Amber tried to smile back, but her heart chilled.

Jack dreamed that he and Bogie stood shadowed by an immense gold-flamed tree, overlooking a river valley that he'd never seen before. The hills were new, sharp and jagged purple, spearing the horizon. Bogie held his hand with a gentle gauntlet and was speaking to him.

"I have to go, Jack."

"Where?"

"Down there. I can hear it calling and I know I have to go."

Jack looked across the valley, to the dark patterns at the base of the mountain peaks. "Why?"

"I can't help it. I've got to go. And you and Amber, too, must come with me. No matter what."

No matter what. No matter what. The white, Flexalinked armor began to walk forward, tugging him insistently after. Jack tried to anchor himself but could not match the armor's strength. He turned and reached into the shadows at his back for help. "Amber!"

She was there and caught his free hand and together they tried to withstand Bogie's march.

But it was no use. The armor uprooted them even as he toppled the golden tree in his path and they were all done for, doomed, as Bogie dragged them after.

Jack bolted upright, his flanks heaving, and he felt a firm hand on his shoulder.

"Easy there, mate. Always was a peculiarly light sleeper."

Jack turned. It was mid-downtime. "What are you doing up, Stash?"

"We all are. I was tryin' to wake you, anyhow. It's time."

He looked around and saw the silhouetted forms of the crew getting up and dressing. "What's going on?"

"A little surprise for our buggy friends."

Boggs knelt by the bunk. "Come on, Jack. Get the armor on. We need you."

Shit. Words dried in Jack's throat. They were going to try to bust out of the mines and go for the laser cannons. Jack knew it as surely as if they'd told him. The orbiting Thrakian ship overhead would be their first target—if they made it that far.

"All of us?"

"All of us, or none. It's the only way, mate."

Jack looked around. Perez was dressed and watching the door for K'rok and the berserker. Dobie and Ron were suiting up and Jack realized they'd brought in deepsuits with them. Bill, Manny and Boggs had hauled out the battle suit and had the seams opened to help him in.

"The charges—"

"All up. I'm good for somethin'," Stash said. He leaned close. "Don't tell me one of the Emperor's own prize boys won't fight for his freedom."

That wasn't it. Jack stared at the armor, afraid to touch it. He hadn't had the time or the nerve to go in and rip the chamois out, his skin recoiling at even the thought of touching it. And what if the berserker wasn't regenerating through the hide? What if it still hatched inside the suit and began to gnaw on him after he thought he was safe?

Boggs whispered sharply, "We've no time to waste."

He couldn't let them all go to their deaths. "All right." He pushed the cover aside and began to suit up.

Bogie knew. He fairly quivered with eagerness. *It's time, boss.*

"Right, you bloodthirsty beggar."

Boggs handed him his helmet. "You know what we're going to do?"

"I've got a fairly good idea. What about K'rok and the berserker?"

"We want you to take them out."

Jack was glad Boggs couldn't see the expression on his face clearly. He only said, "Easier said than done. I'll back you up then, follow and then hold off the trouble as long as I can. Good enough?"

"The best I can ask of anybody." Boggs slapped him on the side of the helmet and turned around to suit himself up.

Live, fight, live, the suit hummed.

"Shut up, Bogie," Jack murmured. He checked his weapons' charges.

Amber woke suddenly, a hand over her mouth. Colin took it away as soon as she recognized him.

"It's time."

"What?" She sat up on the small bed and noticed he was fully suited.

"The diversion I told you about. The Thraks are going to be very busy shortly. Lenska has a power sled with the computer programed with the coords. It's now, or never, as they say."

"But what about—" she stopped. "What if—"

He kissed her gently on the forehead, the way the father she'd never known might have done, if he'd stuck around that long. "You can take care of yourself, and Jack, too, if it comes to that. But I expect you to remember the rules of Christian behavior I've been drumming into you."

"I'll ... try," Amber said softly. Something choked her throat, making it nearly impossible to speak. "What ... what am I supposed to do now?"

"Wait, and pray, I think. Do you believe in God?"

What a terrible thing to ask her, she who'd only dared believe in herself and then Jack. She looked into his deep brown eyes, eyes just as capable of fire as loving mildness. "Sometimes."

"Fate then?"

"Luck."

"As you will. Pray to the luck that has brought us all together at this time and place," he said.

"Never doubt that this was intended." He straightened and left, the lanky aide at his side.

Oh, Jack, Amber thought. *What's going to happen now?*

CHAPTER 18

As they started down the half-lit corridors, Jack thought of all the things he'd meant to do but hadn't had the time. He'd never thought that way before a fight and it bothered him, but he couldn't stop the parade of images through his mind. He'd never been able to go and try to find Fritzi's body and bring it to rest—nor even to tell Gail he'd gone missing. And he hadn't been able to tell Amber what it meant to him that she'd trailed him across space and found him . . . and the feelings for her he was beginning to have. He'd kissed her once, long ago, a first kiss, chaste and fond. Now he'd like to kiss her again and give himself up to the warmth of the response he thought it would bring.

These were not thoughts that went well with starting a small war.

Let me at 'em.

"Not yet," Jack responded. "The ones in front of us are friends." The wave of emotions trying to wrap around him twisted in his gut as well as his mind. Outside of Amber and Jack, did the sentience even know the difference between friend and enemy? The hideous saurian that trailed after K'rok seemed to have no thoughts at all.

The realization of what K'rok had probably gone through to tame the berserker iced down Jack's back. He could not imagine facing down a full-grown berserker long enough to gain a reputation as master and feeder. As he trotted down the corridor, he found himself developing a new respect for the Milot.

His tracking screen flickered an image at him, coming down the side corridor and coming fast. Boggs and Stash and the others had nearly reached the outside lock. Jack checked the screen again. Two blips, both mean and ugly.

"Boggs."

"Yeah, Jack."

"I've got company. Can you blow the airlock?"

He saw them bunch up and then a white-fire flare. The helmet filtered out the glare.

"We've got it. The Sweeper armory is right next door. We'll be picking up weapons there."

"Then I'm dropping off. I'll be busy for a few minutes. You be careful out there." Jack pivoted to block the side corridor, no doubt in his mind that he would be facing the fully armed Milot and his savage berserker. The armor was no protection against the saurian. He'd seen suits torn into shreds from the inside out before. Stay out of reach of that thing, he told himself, and took a defensive stance.

He fired at the shadow rounding the corridor bend, saw a shield go up, and K'rok came round holding a norcite shield and wearing bracers of

Endura, as well as a modified suit from neck to ankle. The huge being braked to a stop and massive eyebrows did a dance of surprise as he faced Jack, his ears coming forward.

"Who be you?" the field commander boomed. At his back, the berserker reared up taller, and its neck fringe began to flare erect.

Jack realized that he might have to bring down the whole building to stop the Milot. He didn't have a field pack on with that much auxiliary power, but he did have enough power to slow the Milot down if he could get a shot clear of the norcite shield. The hesitation brought a comment from K'rok.

"Eh. I have seen your kind before. You should be ground to dust with the rest of my world." He wrinkled his ursine brow, peering at Jack. "You be one of the diggers? Yes, I think so. I sensed one of you be different. Jack, isn't it?"

Jack triangulated a shot off the corridor wall, and the resulting diffused spray rained on K'rok, who jumped back with a barking growl, and a shower of sparks spat and danced off the norcite shield. The berserker made a sound that disrupted in his suit mikes but curdled Jack's blood anyhow.

The fur about his ears still smoking, K'rok craned his neck to look around the shield. He fired back. Jack flinched as the shot broke on the battle armor. He did not even feel the heat. He wondered how far Boggs and the others had gotten.

Jack had no time for further thought as K'rok signaled, firing, even as the saurian charged him.

He let his reflexes go, hit the power vault, and let the beast's own vectoral force spin him away, down the corridor. Before landing, he let off another shot at K'rok, who ducked away.

The Milot showed his teeth. "You and I once be comrades in war, eh, Jack? Now you wonder why I be with the Thraks."

Jack hadn't, but suddenly he knew. "Because you can't survive if you're dead."

"Yes. Basic. My people's survival be my destiny now."

"Then step back. Let me go. I don't want to bring you down." Jack's attention flicked away briefly. The saurian was still quiet on the corridor floor after having slammed into the wall. It was at his back. The last thing he wanted was to have it take him from behind.

K'rok shook his heavy head. "I have to fight, Dominion Knight. My officers ask this of me, to let me survive. You understand? And there is more. Here, on this dead moon, be a secret of the ages. For my people, I will go there and learn it."

"Secret?" Jack watched the Milot closely. At the corner of his attention, he thought he saw the berserker twitch.

"There be something buried in the rock out there—something which my officers be very interested in. What could it be? Why here? I wonder, too. And for this wonderment, I will look."

"You'll have to find a deepsuit big enough," Jack bandied as he realized the Milot was talking about the dig site. What, in God's name, was out there?

K'rok showed his teeth even wider. "You be knowing it, too. I ask you this, fellow warrior. You wear armor from the Sand Wars. I be knowing it well—perhaps I even be knowing you, though I do not understand your youngness. The Thraks took your home and mine. Turned all to sand, to nest for their young. Why? Survival. No young, no people. In this even Thraks like you and me. Thraks are brave warriors. Death dealers. No ones, not me, not you, stopped them until they felt like stopping."

His rear camera screen showed the saurian moving ever so slightly. Gaining consciousness, or gathering for a spring? Jack shifted balance, prepared to react. He should not be listening to K'rok, but he couldn't help it. Here was a barbarian on the scale of galactic civilization, but one who seemed to have thought of answers to some of Jack's questions.

"So tell me this," K'rok said, and his voice became an intimate growl. He lowered the norcite shield slightly. "What made you and me leave our homes? Thraks. Bigger, better warriors. So what made Thraks leave nesting planets of their own?" His eyes seemed to burn through Jack's face plate. "Bigger, better warriors. What be buried out there? Maybe one of the warriors the Thraks fear. They want to know. So do I. If Thraks fear it, then I fear it more. But to fight, it always helps to know enemy better."

Jack had no time to answer, as the berserker growled and hit him, between the shoulders, staggering the battle armor forward. K'rok shouted, "I be leaving, Jack. Good fortune be yours," and turned to disappear down the corridor.

Jack was too busy to watch him leave. The huge creature wrestling him scrabbled at the armor, clawing for a hold, which he was just as determined not to let the berserker get. He felt himself tilted into midair as the saurian prepared to slam him down.

Tear him in pieces, boss.

"Shit," Jack answered. "What the hell do you think he's trying to do to me?" He hit the thrusters and propelled the saurian backward, overbalancing him. The two of them crashed to the floor. Jack felt every square inch of the pressure of the hit. His teeth rattled in their sockets.

He rolled quickly and brought his boot up in the berserker's plated face, kicking into the crimson maw of endless teeth. The gigantic lizard head snapped back with the force. It snapped and growled and came on again.

Jack knew a heart-stopping moment when he was certain he would not be able to stop it—and that Bogie was a brother of this beast. Bile filled his mouth at the thought he could be metamorphosed into an abomination like this. The rage that pumped his own adrenalin and quickened his own reflexes shrank back at the horror he felt. He heard a rending cry, inside his head.

Jack fought a gauntlet free and fired, taking off the berserker's jaws. As blood and flesh spurted, he propelled himself from under the carcass and staggered to his feet.

He would have gone down again, almost immediately, if the Flexalinks hadn't locked.

He shook. He was hurt. Badly. The shock wave of his fall must have scrambled something internally. Maybe broke a couple of ribs. He took a shuddering breath.

Boggs. Stash. Bailey. The rest of Crew Two, waiting for him, out there, to make a run at the laser cannons. Even if the Sweeper armory had yielded some fire power, his was the greater. They waited for a Dominion Knight to help them win their freedom.

K'rok had gone on a mission of his own, perhaps to the dig site. Jack licked his lips and forced the battle armor into a lumbering run. He wasn't finished yet.

And inside his mind, Bogie keened in grief that he was feared and hated instead of loved.

CHAPTER 19

Amber was sitting huddled by the hotel window when the door schussed open abruptly, and a struggling, swearing St. Colin was tossed in by a Thrakian guard. She jumped to her feet and ran to the older man as he bounced off the floor.

She spat at the Thraks, who made an irritated buzzing noise and left the doorway of the room, but the opening was still overwhelmed by the bulky figure standing there. It twisted its helmet off, and her nose was engulfed by its odor. As Colin muttered, "I'm all right," and sat up with her help, the beast ducked down and pushed its way in.

"I be K'rok. Commander Talthos has withdrawn to our orbiting vessel. You be lucky, Walker, that I found you and not he."

Amber, hands shaking, helped Colin up and they both sat on the couch, dwarfed by this towering, shaggy beast. She swallowed tightly. Was this the Milot from the mines? And if he was here, what was happening there? What had happened to Jack?

Colin rubbed the back of his neck.

"What's happened?" She looked desperately from the older man to the Milot and back. If only she had not lost her weapons back on Wheeling.

"The miners have overcome the guards at the laser cannons. It's a pitched battle out there, and the Thraks are losing. We didn't quite make it to the sleds."

"Where's Lenska?"

Colin's face pinched and he shook his head.

"Oh, no." Amber felt her throat catch. "What do you want with us? We won't do you any good as hostages."

"Maybe not." The Milot strode to the window. "The sled you be using, Walker, was destroyed with your man. But you be knowing where to go . . . and I want that information."

"The coords of the site?"

Amber felt Colin stiffen at her side. She clutched his arm. "Don't tell him, Colin. You don't have to. Jack is either dead or taking care of himself."

"Jack?" K'rok's massive head made a small movement, either of surprise or respect. "You be knowing the Knight?"

"Yes."

"Don't say anything more, Amber."

She stared at the Milot intently. She had only one weapon left, one she could make out of herself, and she gathered her mind to do it.

He raised a glove and pointed at her. "You be a warrior, too, if small."

Surprised, she hesitated. Colin held her hands tightly.

The Milot continued, "I have only one more destiny for my people. I must be at the dig site. Give me the information I need."

"Why? What do you want at the site?"

His ursine eyes flickered with hot emotion. "You, Walker, want the dig. Talthos willing to risk war with the Dominion for the dig. People of Lasertown kill themselves, for the dig. What be it that tangles all our survivals together? I must know, for my people. For the Milos that will never be again, and the Milos we hope someday to be."

Colin's grip on Amber relaxed as he half-said to himself, "By God, I was right. There is something uncanny about the site." To K'rok, he added, "You won't damage the evidence?"

"Maybe. Maybe not. But you will be telling me where to go."

"No, no, you don't understand. It's my religion, Milot. I can't let you go out there to—to destroy it all."

Amber drew in a breath and focused on the Milot. He frowned at her, beetle-browed, as though he sensed what she would do.

Colin stood up abruptly. "Take me with you. Let's both go and see what it is."

"Colin!"

"Stay out of this, Amber."

"But he could . . . he could kill you and leave you out there, if he wanted."

Swifter than either of them could imagine, K'rok's hand shot past Colin, knocking him aside, grasping Amber by the throat, and dangling her off her feet. She choked and gasped, her face fiery with the effort of breathing. She lanced all her thought at him, and nothing happened.

The Milot shook her slightly. She gargled for breath and felt her body dance like a puppet. "Small warrior should know not all weapons work the same."

"What's he talking about? Let her go, K'rok. Let her go!"

"You be telling me what I want to know."

Colin walked over to the hotel desk and picked up a form and a pen. Amber coiled to strike a second time.

"Ten degrees and we've got a direct hit!" Dobie's voice inched higher.

"Quiet, mate, you're disrupting my concentration."

Jack backed up to the base of the laser cannon. His gauges were down by half, and he felt himself sucking in each breath harder and harder. By scanner, he swept the range of cold gray stone and dust in front of them, littered with broken forms, some Thrakian and a few human. "I can't hold much longer. Point that thing and fire!"

Boggs sagged against Jack. "They won't be calling me Pops now," the miner said.

"No," Jack answered briefly, his attention on his long-range tracking screen. "That they won't. But if they don't get that ship before it starts a strafing run, they won't be calling any of us by name!"

As Stash made a derisive noise, Jack spotted a

movement by one of the field bunkers the Thraks had thrown together. "Get down!"

Jack picked off the thrower, but not in time to catch the grenade as it hit and bounced, then exploded. More deadly than the shards of its case were the percussions, the sonic forces it expended. Jack staggered back and Boggs was torn from his side, bounding across the terrain.

He recovered and went to the old man. The hiss of the punctured suit obscured his moans. Jack found the leak, a tear in the right ankle, and with a gentle welding beam from his left finger, closed it tightly. "All right, Boggs?"

Feeble gasps answered, then, "Lost some air, boy."

"I know. You'll have to get back to staging as soon as you can."

"Help me up."

Jack gave him a hand up. Stash's deepsuit turned and beckoned to them. Dobie had been torn off the targeting control. "Give me a hand here, mate. Dobie's out cold."

Perez added, "He'll be all right, though, man."

Boggs hobbled to the control and began to reset it. Jack rechecked the long-range screen.

"Shit. Here they come."

Stash must be showing his teeth in that cocky grin of his, he thought, as the New Aussie answered, "All the better. Me range is a little short here."

The laser cannon shifted direction ever so slightly. Then, Stash yelled, "Fire!" and they all ducked away from the blinding glare that their miners' helmets could not screen very effectively.

Only Jack stood to watch the skies split by the glare as the Thrakian warship swept into view.

He whooped with astonishment, then caught his breath sharply, as the cannon scored a solid hit. The ship jumped, and veered, and sheared off, crackling with red and blue fire. Stash stood up. "By god," he said. "I hit it."

Jack saw a lot of movement on his tracking screen. He held up a gauntlet. "I think we've got our reinforcements."

With yells and shouts of joy, breaking up into static over the com lines, the Sweepers broke out of the dome, sled after sled of them, firing sporadically at the few remaining Thraks on the field.

Ron helped Dobie to his feet. They waved their arms in greeting and as the sleds pulled up, the Sweepers leaped off and grabbed up the miners, and the unlikely pairs danced in triumph on the face of the dead moon.

Only Jack saw the Thrakian warship tip the horizon for another run.

"Move it!" he yelled, com line crackling with the force of his command. "Get this gun on a sled and get out of here! Get it into the dome or they're going to destroy it."

The celebration stopped. Silhouettes froze a moment, looking back over the jagged moonscape, then hustled into vigorous motion. The movable base of the laser cannon was disconnected, tools and gloves weaving in an economy of motion. To prevent its destruction, it was going back inside the domes, where it was hoped the Thraks would hesitate to destroy the fragility of life.

"Move it, move it!"

With the precision of a drill team, they hoisted the weapon onto one of the sleds. It sagged, hovers whining to hold the extra weight. Jack waved at the miners. "Run for it, dammit! The sleds will never hold all of us!"

They broke into a dead run for the domes, Sweepers and diggers alike. Jack watched them go, his ribs stabbing with every breath, and he lumbered into motion behind them. Despite the power, he could not keep up. His guts wrenched with agony and he fought to keep air in his lungs. Something wet dribbled from his chin. He tasted the flat, metallic taste of blood in his mouth.

The dome air lock yawned darkly in front of them, welcoming the first sled, and then the second with the cannon, and then the third burgeoning with personnel. He saw Boggs stagger in, and Bailey and Perez, too. All of the deepsuits made it, as the black shadows of the Thrakian warship swept over him, and reflexively, Jack dove to the surface of the moon.

It seemed to hang over him, black death, the suit mikes catching the screams of its drives.

Then, it veered away at the last second, leaving the domes of Lasertown intact.

As Jack lurched to his feet, he caught a sobbing breath as the bulkhead slammed shut. He managed a shambling run. "Let me in!"

His com answered only with static. He curled

a gauntlet and pounded. No one came to open up for him.

He pointed a finger and then dropped his hand with a cruel laugh as the norcite shielding on the air lock mirrored his futile image back at him. Jack sank to the dust, locked outside, too hurt to fight any longer.

CHAPTER 20

Jack. Get up, Jack.

He hurt. Gods, he hurt. And he was cold, too, something he rarely had to worry about in the suit. That's why he wore the chamois at his back, to help catch the sweat that usually trickled down his bare skin, and to keep the circuitry of the armor from chafing when he wore a field pack. The chamois lay limp across him now, for he was facedown in the dust, and cold.

Come on, Jack. We've got to go.

He twisted a little in the armor, leads crimping, and then made the suit roll with him, roll so he could get up again. His whole body protested with sharp, jabbing pains that brought a groan to his lips. He'd taken too much punishment lately. He couldn't take any more.

Sure, you can, boss. Come on or we're going to be late.

Jack recoiled from that mindtouch with the realization of what it was he was hearing. Berserker. Like that miscreant he'd killed at the mines. Spawn of a miscreant which would cannibalize him soon, metamorphosing them into a . . . a thing that knew only to eat and kill or be killed.

No, boss.

"Don't deny it. You *can't* deny it. You saw it yourself, through me." Jack leaned against the dome. He balled his gauntlet into a fist and pounded one last time. Looking up, he saw laser fire scoring against the sheeting and blackened junk that used to be a security camera system once upon a time. They couldn't even see him to know he was out here. He shook his head once, slowly, to clear it.

Let me help you, boss.

Jack stiffened. The mindtouch encircled him intimately, a whiskery fine touch over skin and bones and muscle and blood inside. He thrust back angrily and the touch withdrew quickly as though shocked. "Leave me alone. You can have me when I'm dead, not before." He wobbled away from the useless bulkhead. He could circle the domes. He knew there were other air locks, other entrances. Surely he could find someone or something to acknowledge his presence and let him in.

Gently, but strongly, *No, boss.*

The suit locked to a halt despite Jack's movement inside of it. He gasped with the pain of stopping.

We have to go. Slowly, the suit pivoted and reeled away from the dome, in a different direction.

"No. There's nothing out there. This place is dead, Bogie, and so am I if I don't get inside!"

Sorry, Boss. Got to go. I can help you if you let me—

"No!"

Then you'll just have to come as far as you can.

Without his volition or direction, the suit jerkily began to stride across the landscape. His legs moved swiftly without his telling them to, trapped within seven league boots of armor he could no longer control. He was answering the siren call that had led so many others to death whether he wanted to or not.

The entity Amber had once described as a baby, parasitic and selfish, had now come into its own. Jack could no longer dominate it. As he'd seen it happen on Milos, Jack was approaching the beginning of the end. As the suit began to take the lunar landscape in leaps and bounds, he threw back his head and screamed, but there was no one human to hear it. "Let me go!"

Boggs came to with his suit stripped down to his waist and an IV in his arm. He blinked. The medic standing over him looked anything but sympathetic. Boggs tried his mouth to see if it, at least, still worked. "Did everybody get in?"

"I guess. You'd better take it easy, Pops. That heart isn't what it used to be."

"Or the rest of me, either." He lay back, sweat trickling across his bald pate. "Who came in?"

"About twenty of you guys. I guess," and the medic shrugged, "we owe you diggers."

Boggs' chest swelled a little. "I guess you do," he said, and turned his head quietly to rest. His eyesight swept across the pile of deepsuits in the bay. There was no armor standing in the corner. He looked back to the medic. "Hey—you!"

"C'mon, old man. Thought I told you to take it easy. We'll have someone take you to ICU in a couple of minutes."

"No, no, wait. Where's the guy in the battle armor? Sandy hair, blue eyes ... knows what he's doing."

"Nobody like that came in. Some mouth with black hair changed suits for a fresh one and left again. That's it."

Boggs closed his eyes again, this time tightly, feeling too old to cry. Jack hadn't made it. He'd known Jack was hurt, but not complaining. Well, that field of rocks out there between the mines and the domes had claimed some of the best. As something akin to agony squeezed at his heart again, he lay very still.

Amber opened her eyes. Colin leaned over her, holding her chilled hand in his warm one. "Are you all right, child?"

She sat up with a jerk, expecting to see the Milot's body stretched out beside her, knowing the psychic energy with which she'd finally lashed at him. But there was no sign of K'rok. "He must have a thick skull," she muttered, as Colin helped her to stand. Her knees threatened to buckle and he slid a chair under her.

"Can you breathe?"

Her throat felt as though it had been ripped open. He passed a glass of water to her and she sipped at it gingerly. "Yes, but it hurts." She fingered her throat, feeling puffiness, and knew she must be purpling already. Her voice was a whispery husk of its normal pertness when she asked, "Did you tell him?"

"Yes. It served no further purpose to hide it from him." Colin rubbed his hands together. His knuckles were thickened and as she looked at them, she saw the tiny scars of someone who'd either worked hard or fought hard.

"What'd you think he'll do?"

"I don't know. He may well destroy the site after he's examined it, but somehow—I don't think so. No. I envision him as a gladiator determined to make a last stand, but against whom or why—"

"Thraks."

"Maybe. If they wanted to, they could have hit it anytime. No, I think they want to examine it fully before they do." Colin stood up, rubbing his jaw. "Perhaps now is not a good time, but—"

Her senses tingled. "For what?" she shot back, looking up.

"The miners have overrun the Thraks. I'm told they got hold of the laser cannon and caused some considerable damage. The warship has pulled back, to a more distant orbit. Lasertown is back under Dominion control again."

Amber would have grinned, but something in the Walker's demeanor told her this was not a cause for celebration. "What happened? Where's Jack?"

"They told me it was a heroic effort—"

She pushed herself to her feet. The cords on

her neck constricted with pain and grief, and she brushed it away. "Tell me what happened!"

"They're not sure. The miners who survived brought the cannon into the domes, playing the odds that the Thraks wouldn't hit us and cause a major incident. Jack didn't make it. There's an old man in ICU, by the name of Boggs—"

"We know him. You and I met him when we got stuck down there. He's the shift supervisor. What happened to him?"

"Heart attack. He'll be all right, but he says Jack ran into K'rok and the berserker covering their escape from the mines. He said Jack seemed to be hurt ... heard him breathing hard over the com lines, but Jack kept on fighting. And when they had to make a run for the domes, Jack didn't follow. He's locked out, Amber."

"He's not dead. I know it."

Colin looked at her kindly. She thrust out, pushing back his sympathetic hand, and turning away. "I know he's not dead."

"Maybe not. If you're well enough, I'm going to go down to the locks. They need people with deepsuit experience to help bring the bodies back in. I'm hoping I won't find Jack down there."

Amber didn't say good-bye. She couldn't. Her throat ached as if it would burst. She heard the door open and close behind Colin. As it closed, she let herself fall back onto the chair. She curled up and opened up her mind, searching desperately.

"Bogie, stop. I can't go much farther." Jack reeled back in the suit, feeling his muscles go,

258

sagging. But he had the feeling that even if he passed out, the armor would carry him onward.

The suit staggered to a halt. *Boss, let me touch you.*

"No!"

You gave me life, Jack.

He closed his eyes. The stilted mindtouch was gone, matured into communication that was undeniable. He wanted to thrust it away and could not. It burned through his brain like a hard wire. "Get out of me," he said.

Let me help.

Behind his closed eyelids, the monstrous image of the berserker flared into sight.

"Jeezus," Jack said wearily. "You just want to keep me alive long enough to—to—"

Boss!

Jack opened his eyes at the hurt. Feelings? Now the sentience had feelings? If only Amber were here. He chinned off the holograph field and pulled an arm carefully back out of the sleeve. He touched his flat stomach. The skin was icy. He probed gently and the resounding burst of pain made him gasp and nearly double over, except that the armor caught and held him.

Bogie said, *Boss, we've got to go. If you won't let me heal you . . . I've got to go anyway. There's no more time.*

"No. You're not going anywhere. I've turned off the field." Jack laughed softly, bitterly. "I'm going to die here, standing up in this thing, and when you do hatch, you've got nothing but vacuum to hatch into."

Jack. Please turn the holo back on.

"No." Jack tilted his head back, resting it against the circuitry and chamois at the back of the suit. "I want it this way."

For the tiniest past of a second, he felt a fluttering touch, not Bogie, but terribly familiar.

They both said simultaneously, "Amber?"

Amber?

And then the touch was gone.

It spurred Bogie. *Jack!*

Before he could answer no again, it gripped him. He clenched his teeth and felt the inexorable pressure on his neck and skull. "Bogie. What the hell are you going?"

Turning the holo back on, Jack.

It pushed his face into the switching and the rosy field came back on.

With a jerking movement, his arm went back into the sleeve. Jack clenched his fist, thinking momentarily of turning his weapons on himself.

I wouldn't do that, Jack. Just remember that where there's life, there's hope.

Jack smothered a groan as the armor reeled back into movement. Then he spotted a blip on his short-range tracking. Turning his head slightly, he saw other signals coming in on his long-range. The long-range told him that the Thraks were moving again.

And something else was out there in space, besides.

Amber lurched back in her chair, holding her throat with both hands, trying to soothe the pain of her injury. Hot tears slid down her face.

He was alive, she knew that, and in the grip of Bogie's madness. There was nothing she could do for him. Nothing. Her influence had gone the way of Jack's. The battle armor was carrying him away from the domes and to his death and there was nothing she could do but wait.

She scrubbed away the tears. Then wait she would. Because the Bogie she'd touched had a curious feeling for Jack even as it forced him across the dead moon landscape on a mission of madness. She had to believe that it fought its own will to survive, had fought it for months, not wishing to feed off Jack any more than Jack wanted to be consumed. It grew to life, slowly, painstakingly, linked to Jack by something it could not comprehend.

She prayed it was love.

Jack snapped to with a sudden awareness, like a second wind. He discounted his alertness, having seen it before in dying men. But it stood him in good stead now as the short-range tracking screen showed him a blip just around the sharp crest of rocks they were rounding.

"Bogie," he said. "We're not alone. Give me back control. Whatever it is, is lying in ambush, and you don't have the finesse yet to face it. If you want to get where you're going, you're going to have to give back control *now*."

The armor staggered, and then Jack felt command return to him again. He moved quickly, tacking to the right, but it was too late.

The sled with the black-suited driver came piling at them. Jack hit the power vault. It drove him up, though not quite as high as he'd planned and Jack realized he was running close to a red field. He fired downward and the jolt rocked the sled, dumping the driver in the dust. The sled nosed to a halt among the rocks.

The driver lay facedown, quiet, as Jack landed and approached. His side ached again and he hoped he hadn't spent what meager reserve he had left. Beyond the black-suited man, he saw the widening expanse of a massive chasm, and realized that Bogie had brought him nearly to what must be the Walker site. He looked down at the driver. Another victim?

As he leaned down, the man lashed out, kicking. Jack rocked back, gasping at the blow to his midriff. The armor toppled and went down. A moment later, the man jumped him, and Jack felt all the wind and life go out of him. Their face plates clicked.

"Hello, mate," Stash said cheerfully. "Thought you was left for dead back there."

"Not . . . quite," Jack wheezed.

"Yeah? Well, this must be what they call serendipity. You see, I was a bit upset about losing you. You stood to make a great deal of money for me. Now they wanted you alive, but I suppose they'll take dead as well. After all, that's what you were supposed to be, wasn't it, now? Dead as a burned-out chip. But you got chilled down instead and sent off to Lasertown. Don't go runnin' off like poor Fritzi, Jack. I scouted his body back there a ways. I'm going to be leaving you here, mate. I can tell from your face and the sound of your breathing that you ain't going anywhere. I'll be back."

"Where?"

"Over yonder. I have a little job to do. Me original job. A demo job, and then a hit. Took me a while to get out here without causing suspicion, but I made it."

"The . . . the dig."

"Right again. You're a regular comet. But I knew that the moment I saw you. Knew you was something special and I could make a fortune off you." Stash made a clicking sound. "Life is beautiful sometimes when it all comes together, ain't it? I'll get a fair chunk of credit for blowin' the site, and then when I bring you in, I can guarantee th' old Walker'll be weepin' at your side, and it'll just be a touch to take him out. And then I'll take your body on for another chunk of credit. What a job this was. Worth bein' chilled down for a couple of months, mate."

Stash moved, looking up. After a moment, he bent down again, the face plates nudging. "Want to know something else? I never was in your Guard. You ain't quite got it all back yet, Jack, after cold-sleep fever. Now you won't have the time to get it. Rum deal for you. When th' the word filtered down about what my employer was lookin' for in Lasertown, I knew it had to be you. You was worth all the trouble I took lookin' out for you. But Winton told me all about you, you see, and he'll be happy to get delivery. Got to run, mate. You just lie still and wait for me. If you can hold on, I'll get some help for you. Winton told me he'd just as soon have you in the flesh. Says you're a hard man to kill and he'd like to get his hands on you. But he'll pay either way. So it's up to you, mate. Too bad you wrecked the sled. It's wedged itself in pretty good."

Jack felt his sleeve being lifted and knew that he was being tied to the sled. He was too cold to move or to protest.

"See ya, mate. No hard feelings." Stash stood up, moving out of Jack's sight.

In a matter of seconds, the mikes could no longer pick up the scrunch of his footsteps across the rock and ash. Jack watched the short-range screen until his eyelids were too heavy to hold up.

His last thoughts were of Amber and, oddly enough, of Bogie.

Jack. Bogie probed the coldness within his shell. It frightened him. Cold was dormancy to him. He didn't want to go back to being dormant. He needed Jack. Jack's bright, fiery life. His thoughts and his emotions. And because of those other things beyond flesh, Bogie had fought not to grow in the way his kind hungered to grow. He would not rend Jack. He would not!

But he wasn't strong enough to refuse all instincts. The call he must answer. That he could not refuse, for he was still too young and weak. And so, though he smelled the congealing blood and felt the icing body, Bogie moved to do what Jack would not let him do earlier.

He flowed into Jack and moved along the pathways, searching for damage he could repair. He would grow for Jack instead of for himself.

Colin straightened up. Emmanuel took the exhausted deepsuit from him and made ready to suit him up in a fresh one. The Walker looked at his aide, a man who'd been waiting many months for him to come so that the site could be documented. Emmanuel and Lenska had gone through seminary together. The small, slight man showed dark marks under his eyes and already gray flecked his auburn temples. Colin hesitated, for he knew that the aide would do whatever was asked of him, and he wondered for a moment if he was going to ask too much, but he had no choice.

"Send word back to my rooms to the young lady there. Her name's Amber. Tell her we were unable to find the body."

"Yes, sir."

"Then suit up. Get the others together."

Emmanuel's eyebrows went up. Colin snapped, "And hurry. We haven't any time to waste. Before the Thraks come back in or someone gets some efficient martial law established, I want us out at that dig site. You told me you had everything ready to go."

"Yes, sir!" Emmanuel scampered off as Colin fumbled with the interior plumbing of the deepsuit. He had only a moment's hesitation as he decided how he was going to deal with the Milot-Thrakian field commander when he got there.

He would wait no longer. The site was his to document. He had hesitated enough and nearly lost it all.

He would hesitate no longer.

CHAPTER 21

Bogie grew desperate. He could mend here and bypass there, but the spark he searched for he could not find, the spark that set off the fiery essence he'd come to know as his boss. He chased after it, calling, frightened, knowing that his own time of dormancy was growing close if he could not halt Jack's slide into death.

He stopped. Amber. Amber could help. Amber touched him as well, but she was more than fire to him. He could not explain it. And now he went in search of Amber, calling her.

"Bogie." Amber's eyes snapped open at the tentative mental call. She reined him in vigorously. "Bogie, what are you doing out there! You're killing Jack." She caught the fear and iciness of his sentience and felt an echo of it inside her. Where was Jack? At her wonderment, he caught her up and drew her into Jack. With a gasp, she followed.

* * *

Jack woke. Bogie and Amber nudged at him, driving him. He ached all over and gooseflesh ridged his skin. With the square of his chin, he kicked up the heat in the suit. He lay still a moment, lost in his dreams, waiting for the warmth to revive him.

He was still hurt, but something had happened while he was under. He withdrew a hand and rubbed the flat of his torso, wincing under his self-examination. No swelling. Internal bleeding had stopped or he'd be dead. Maybe he was dead.

He took a deep breath and felt the stab of half-mended ribs. If Bogie had finally gone in, he'd done a hell of a job.

"Don't bitch, Jack. He did the best he could."

"Amber?" Jack tilted his head up, looking around, in spite of himself.

"Right. Look for me. Jack, I'm in Lasertown. Where the hell are you?"

He sat up. The Flexalinks complained slightly. The gauges were holding their own, but barely. He might just get out of this alive. He looked out across the lunar valley. "Amber," he said slowly, "I'm overlooking the dig site. It's incredible."

Her answer faded beyond his grasp. "Amber?"

"Jack, Bogie's losing me. I can't . . . can't hold on much longer. Get up, Jack. You're still badly hurt. Get up and get moving. Come back."

Jack aimed carefully and fired the binding fastening him to the sled. He remembered Stash playing Winton's game and that he would ultimately be going after St. Colin. "I'll be back later, Amber, but I've got something to do first. Colin with you?"

"No, he's . . ." she faded again.

"You get hold of him and watch him. Stash is no digger, he's a terminator. If he gets by me, he's after Colin. Take care of it, okay?"

"Jack!"

The noise of the suit power lifting the sled out of the rocks drove Amber out of his mind. Jack leaned over and hit the starter. It vibrated into life under his gauntlets.

"All right, Bogie. Let's take a look at what's caused all this trouble."

Right, Boss.

As Jack descended into the depression of the site, he could see the shapes of machinery left idle under mylar blankets. A few mini-domes had been set up. Two had been pressurized, he could tell by the faint droplets of humidity condensing on the interior. There was no immediate sign of Stash, but Jack found a good-sized target blip moving onto his scanner.

And a second one, motionless within the nearest dome. Jack moved the sled into position and damped down the hovers, letting it settle near the air lock. He opened it, waited for the cycle, and damn near tripped over the bulk of K'rok, facedown on the dome flooring and tied up like an interstellar delivery. The Milot wiggled vigorously.

Jack took off his helmet and breathed deeply. The air in the mini-dome was the best he'd breathed in months, even with the rankness of the Milot's body oils. K'rok's helmet lay a few feet away.

The Milot glared at him and thumped his boots on the flooring. Jack smiled. "I think you're better off that way. Who got you? Stash?"

The Milot's eyes flickered, slightly reddish. The jowls tightened stubbornly.

Jack shrugged. "All right. Have it your way. He's out there somewhere, planting charges even now. He's been hired to blow this place sky-high."

K'rok huffed.

Jack bent down and pulled the gag off. "Better?"

"Yes. The warrior does not fight honorably."

"I'd say that. But what about you and me? If I untie you, is it going to be another battle? I've got business here and I don't want you in my way. Stash is mine, and you're going to have to ally with me if you want to save this dig."

The Milot considered him. "We were allied once before, you and I."

"Yeah, and as far as my memory goes, that didn't work out too well." Jack turned to go. "Maybe I'll do this on my own."

"Wait!" K'rok fairly bounced inside his ropes. "I will help you."

"Swear on it?"

"By the destiny of my people," the Milot said.

Jack smiled gently. He knew that was as good an oath as he was going to get, but he also knew that the Milot would stand by it. He bent down to loosen the bindings. He almost had K'rok loose when a tremendous boom shook the entire dome. Jack tossed K'rok's helmet at him as the Milot kicked free. The mini-dome's clouded interior hid the outside and Jack ducked through the air lock and waited impatiently for the cycle to let him outside.

They hit the ground and rolled as a second blast sent shock waves over the horizon. He looked up to see the Thrakian warship screaming out of orbit, a second ship at its heels.

K'rok tapped him on the shoulder as the view of the space battle drew Jack in and he tried to ID the second vehicle. The Milot pointed, and Jack saw the silhouetted form of Stash as he paced along a bluff and he recognized the stop, drill, and implant routine. The Thraks breezed down, front lasers firing. Stash dove for cover behind a steeplelike boulder, and Jack could hear the crackle of a com line not on his frequency but close enough to cause interference. The second warship came whistling in on the tail of the Thraks, firing back.

Jack looked back up. The warships played tag on the far horizon. Stash looked up and then stood, either unnerved or—

Supported by the second ship. The ID of that ship nagged at Jack. He almost knew it. . . .

The Milot made a sound that Jack recognized from his months of duty in the Sand Wars. In spite of himself, he grinned at the curse.

K'rok began to crawl forward, stalking the terminator. He ducked down as sleds veered suddenly into view, crawling with deepsuits, and Jack did not recognize them as either friend or foe. The sleds hovered to a stop by the far dome.

A man got off. "Hello," he broadcast toward Stash, unaware of his danger.

Jack recognized Colin's sainted tones. He vaulted to his feet, yelling, "Colin, get down! That man's a killer!"

Bogie pumped him. He bounded across the landscape and barreled into the deepsuit, pushing Colin out of harm's way as Stash aimed and fired.

The lightweight pocket laser beam merely grazed the battle armor. Jack righted himself and faced Stash across the excavation, his heart pounding and ears roaring, and a deadly calm pervading all his decisions.

"What is this, Jack?"

Over the lines, he could hear Stash tuning in as he answered the Walker, "His employers don't intend to let you view the site, Colin. Or to let you live to leave Lasertown."

"Now, mate," Stash soothed. "You might be givin' the saint here a prejudicial viewpoint of me. Besides, you're a bit too late. I've planted all the charges I need. But I can always make a deal."

"Don't listen to him," Jack warned. His long-range tracking screen flashed a gentle warning. The warships were heading back. He had no time for words.

He jumped Stash. The man in the deepsuit went rolling, bounded back to his feet, and responded with a lashing kick that rocked the battle armor back. Jack knew then that he'd gravely underestimated Stash all the time he'd spent with him. Under the cocky, abrasive New Aussie veneer lay a quiet and efficient killer.

Battle armor or not, Stash was not afraid of him. Before Jack could gather himself, the terminator had lashed out again, and the Flexalinks groaned under the assault. Jack swung, ready to fire, then saw that the overspray would set off the demolitions. He hesitated, and Stash lunged at his ankles.

With every spin and blow, Jack had to give way. The pounding on the armor reverberated throughout his barely healed and wracked frame. The suit ground low on power as the two circled each other, and he heard Stash's low laugh.

"Got to think of yourself as invincible, eh, mate."

"Maybe. How do you think of yourself?"

"Good at what I do." Stash lashed out. Jack responded with a short burst that singed the side of the deepsuit helmet, but its effect was more visual than harmful. The weight of the armor began to hang on him.

Stash laughed. "Get me and you're still done for, all of you. The timers are set. Who's going to be defusing them? You're running out of time. My friends are headed back this way. I've got what they want and they're not likely to leave me here alone."

Colin interjected, "Give up and come back with us. Is this worth your life?"

"It's not going to cost me my life, mate. You, maybe." And with that, Stash dodged and fired, passing Jack by.

* * *

But Jack had leaped and the white armor collided with the black deepsuit, sending the beam awry as Jack grasped Stash's wrist and squeezed, pinching the weapon out. The man let out a cry of anguish, going to his knees. Blood gushed from the punctured deepsuit which was no match for the strength of Jack's gauntlet.

The warships came screaming over, the rocks vibrating with their speed and massive power. Locked together, they tumbled and fell, then the Thrakian ship broke away, firing, and the second ship exploded into fiery scrap above them in a deep velvet sky.

Colin let out an involuntary gasp. Jack looked downward at Stash, who lay writhing in the ash as both his air and his blood bled away. He aimed and lasered off the end of the wound, sealing flesh and suit. Stash fainted dead away.

Colin got to his feet, and his aides unfroze from the sleds. "The Thraks, at least, want this site. We have work to do and not much time to do it in. I want those mines defused."

The aides scattered to do his bidding.

K'rok's massive bulk ranged up beside Jack. The Milot touched face plates with Stash and then removed something from the outside mining pouch. It was a small, gray leather square. Jack started to say something, then saw the Thrakian ship wheel over the horizon.

Over his com lines, he heard another frequency crackle once again. He homed in on it. He did not understand the Thrakian language, but he knew a firing sequence and coords when he heard it.

"They're coming in! Get those sleds moving and get out of here."

"What?"

Jack picked up Colin and threw him bodily on the sled. He grabbed at the Milot. "Come on, K'rok. This is going to blow one way or another."

"But-but," stammered the Walker. "Why?"

"It appears that, if the Thraks can't have it, no one can. And, after having blown a Dominion needler out of the sky, they don't seem to want any witnesses," Jack answered, his memory clicking back into place and finally identifying the second warship. "Come on, move it!" His blood chilled as Bogie fought him desperately, not wanting to leave the site.

K'rok jumped the sled. It hovered into power. The first two sleds took off, but the third bowed under their weight. Jack picked up Stash and slung him over his shoulder.

"Jack! Amber will have my hide if I leave you out here."

"I've got a sled by the domes. Get going!" His com lines began to vibrate with the noise of the Thrakian ship moving in.

He began to run, taking the dead moon in leaps and bounds, death itself on his heels. The first mine went off, showering him with rocks and gravel. He jumped the sled and kicked it into power.

As it flared on, he swung it out after the Walkers and followed them out of the valley, to the ridge beyond.

Bogie keened in his mind. Colin stopped the

second sled at the ridge and Jack slewed to a stop behind him.

"Get out of here!"

"No. Not quite yet." The Walker swiveled on the seat, looking back at the dig. "There is something there, just below the surface. Perhaps I'll have a chance to see it yet."

Bogie wailed in Jack's thoughts.

He geared the sled down and held it in idle beside Colin and the two silent Walker aides flanking him. The Thrakian ship swept over and two massive blasts shook the moon.

The bluff opened up, a layer of wall just sliding away from it.

And there, cut into the rock, imprisoned by time and death, reared a creature. A massive, gray, leathern creature as different from a berserker as a man was from a monkey.

Bogie wept.

"What, in god's name, is that?" whispered one of the Walkers.

"Something," Colin said, "that we may just have gone to war over."

Jack saw K'rok move. "Something," the Milot field commander said, "to make even the Thraks afraid."

One of the aides murmured, "It called us to our deaths."

No, Jack, Bogie sobbed. *It called to be free, to live again.* Jack stirred, driven by Bogie's torment. "What is it, Bogie," Jack asked. "What is it?"

I think—me, the sentience answered.

The Thrakian ship looped and came down

again, and as the ground erupted from the chains of mines planted below, the Thraks blasted it from above, powdering the bluff and all the area around it. The thing, whatever it had been, was gone. A high keening noise cut through Jack's mind like a cold wind, and then Bogie, too, was silent.

K'rok was the first to stir. He reached from Colin's sled and thumped Jack. "There be no time to lose," he said.

"Why?"

"They will not stop here. They will take out Lasertown, too. No witnesses. They will blast until nothing is left of this moon but a cloud of dust."

"Good God," Colin said.

But K'rok's words struck Jack through the blackness of his mind that Bogie had left.

He shook his head. "Amber!" He kicked the sled into gear. "We've got time before they re-charge and set up."

"Jack, my warrior friend. The laser cannon is down. There be no way to defend the domes against a direct attack," K'rok sympathized.

"Not if I can help it!" He punched in the homing coords and the sled shot off, flying toward Lasertown. The broken landscape of the dead moon flashed below him. He didn't care if Colin or the others followed him. What he had to do, he would do best alone anyway.

Alone except for Bogie, and that touch was dead, cold, gone beyond his reach. Jack probed gingerly for it even as the sled whined and dodged as he bullied it beyond its top speed. He felt alone without Bogie and knew now what Bogie had not had the ability to tell him.

The alien had not been a killer, after all, not even in the selfish, instinctive way a parasite kills to live. He had been something more, perhaps as novel a creature as was mummified in that cliff. Growing from a scrap of skin, who knew what Bogie was destined to be? Not a berserker. Jack knew that now. K'rok's berserker had no more been capable of thought or feelings than a rock. That was not Bogie.

Just as Amber was not, consciously, capable of being a terminator as Stash had been, though she shrank from her mental abilities. Bogie was gone now, because Jack had not understood and responded in time.

He'd be damned if he was going to lose Amber as well!

By the time he reached the laser-scored air lock, he had his course of action mapped out.

He jumped the sled and left it nosed up to the dome. He picked up Stash's limp form. Groans filled his com line as he shouldered the weight. He patted the New Aussie down.

A bulky knot in the right thigh pocket. Jack opened it up. A tiny, but deadly, explosive. He gave a satisfied nod, slapped it against the norcite seal, backed up and blew the air lock.

He heard the thin whine of alarms as he walked back through the smoking hole. Stash stirred as Jack dropped him. The terminator rolled over, whining, cradling his ruin of an arm.

Jack picked up the laser cannon.

Stash sat up. "What the hell are you doing?"

"Saving your worthless hide. I suggest you crawl back through the bay and see if you can find someone to help you. The other sleds are due here any second. I don't think they're going to slow down if they find you in their way."

Jack hefted the cannon over his shoulder, turned on his heels and left through the gaping hole in the air lock bay. The Thraks knew the cannon had been taken down. They knew they would be coming in for a shot at a helpless dome community.

With a grim smile, he ran across the death-pocked field of gray stone between the dome and the power base for the cannon.

The difference between a good soldier and a dead one was the ability to know the limits of your suit and weapons—and the ability, as well, to strip down and repair what you had as quickly as you could.

His long-range screen blinking danger, Jack worked as quickly as he could. There was no time to reinstate the base, but he stripped down the power cables and hard wired them. Then he stood and reset the cannon on his shoulder. He got firing coords from his suit computer. A little bit bigger than a field pack and with a hell of a lot more power, but the firing trajectory shouldn't be much different. He stood and waited for the Thraks to come within range.

The two sleds zoomed past, and he saw St. Colin skew around on the seat to look at him.

"Good-bye, Jack. God be with you," came the man's voice faintly over the lines.

Jack did not reply. He kept his gaze on the horizon and his tracking screen, praying only that the Thraks did not reverse their direction and come in from the other side.

He wished that he were not quite as alone as he had to be.

About the time adrenalin shock set in, the Thraks showed up in his visual. He began to squeeze his finger on the firing trigger. The fact that the cannon might well blow up and take him with it as well as the Thraks bothered him not a little.

So he thought of Amber as he took aim. Streetwise, beautiful Amber, alone and vulnerable in that dome, waiting for him to come back. Amber, like all of Lasertown, as perishable as a flower on a Thrakian sand planet.

The Thrakian warship swooped in, fearless, sure of its target.

Jack's hand closed. The laser cannon fired. He was aware of only two things: his own cannon's explosion and the explosion of the Thrakian ship a split second after, knocking him on his back.

Then all went still and dark. As he went under, he grabbed one last time for Bogie's sentience, asking it for help.

CHAPTER 22

"Don't you ever try anything like that again."

Amber's face faded in, bleached white by the hospital lights surrounding his gaze. He blinked, then pried heavy eyelids open one more time. He croaked, "That thing packs a kick."

"Yes, I imagine it does. The Thraks thought so, too." Colin perched on the end of the sterile crechelike bed. "Thank you once again for saving this somewhat overrated hide." He patted Jack on his knee. "They've got you wired up here, but I'm told you'll be out tomorrow. Pepys has sent an escort ship to bring you back."

Amber broke in, "You may patronize him if you wish, but I intend to kick the crap out of him the minute he can get out of bed."

"Amber!"

Jack found a chuckle even though it hurt. "It's all right, Colin. She's usually a lot tougher on me than that."

The Walker looked down at him as he stood. "Well. All the same, I owe the two of you a lot. I have some work to do, or I'd not be saying good-bye now. Pepys ordered me home as well, but I take orders from a higher authority than his."

"Work?" Jack found his mouth was about the only part of him that did not ache beyond tolerance.

"I have to make sure the site has truly been destroyed. That means I have a few square kilometers of dust and ash to sift. A few weeks, perhaps. Not much more than that." He sighed. "I still don't understand all that happened here."

"I'm not sure I do either. Stash was working for a group that wanted the site destroyed. His cover was contract labor. Sooner or later, he'd have been on a crew excavating the site. That same group brought in the Dominion needler to harass the Thraks after Governor Franken lost control of the site and Lasertown to the Bugs. From there, I don't know. This is pretty far out for a Dominion ship. At the same time, the Thraks were intensely interested in gaining access to the site themselves. Plus, the mining operation and norcite ore would help defray their expenses."

"But why take me out?"

"Perhaps, St. Colin of the Blue Wheel, for the same reason Pepys fears you. A religious empire can be built just as easily as a political or a military empire. Walkers have the capability of stringing a web of influence."

Colin grimaced. "The last thing we want."

"Ambitious men see ambition in others. It's what they're familiar with and fear most."

"Mmm. And the Thraks, of course, once they'd lost the site and destroyed the needler, feared the political backlash themselves. It would be better to destroy this moon than to face an inquiry."

"They were counting on the slowness of response time of Dominion forces this far out," Jack agreed.

Amber tossed her head, throwing her hair back off her shoulders. "Who sabotaged the tunnels when we flew in?"

"That, I don't know. We'll probably never know."

"And I don't understand what K'rok was doing."

"K'rok's the one who gave me the sense of this whole thing. You're too young to know about the Sand Wars, Amber, but I think Colin here remembers them." Jack gave Amber a warning look before he smiled mildly at the Walker.

"Remember them? I was damn near in them. Ah, Amber. See what you've done to my vocabulary."

"The most peculiar thing about the Sand Wars was that the Thrakian aggression was unprovoked. They just swept into our regions and took over planets, turning them into uninhabitable nests for their young. We thought it was their typical militaristic aggression. The Dominion fought, but couldn't stop them. They stopped when they wanted to, and signed treaties. But it was K'rok who made sense of it. He felt that a bigger, better warrior had driven the Thraks out of their own territory. I tend to agree."

"Was it one of those creatures we saw in the wall?"

"A race of them, perhaps. Or something different. The Thraks didn't have a chance to excavate and find out. But rather than give up the secret to us, they eventually destroyed it."

Amber had been sitting stubbornly silent. She said, "What wall?"

"The bluff of the site. Just as it was destroyed, we got a look at what it was that everyone wanted a look at."

"And?"

Jack shook his head. "Indescribable."

Her lips pouted. Colin shook himself. He patted Jack's knee again. "Well, my boy. The machinations astound me. All the wheels within wheels. Not to mention your being here."

Jack shrugged. "That was totally an accident. I'm supposed to be dead. I have enemies who paid a good deal to see that happened. But the terminator got greedy and sold me as a contract laborer for a bit more money. So I was chilled down and ended up here where it just so happened I could do a lot of damage."

"No accident," Colin told him. "Believe me. Little of that much consequence is accidental. Good luck to both of you. Amber, look me up if you ever wish to become a Walker. I could use someone with your intelligence and guts." With that, the man left the hospital cubicle.

Amber sat quietly with her head tilted to one side, as if listening to his departure, before she pounced.

Jack winced. "Not there. That hurts."

"You ass. There isn't anything that doesn't hurt on you. But what about Bogie? You should be dead, but the medics pried you out and found you healing before their very eyes. And don't you give me that look. We had the room swept electronically before they installed you in here."

But Amber's words had warmed him. Jack grasped her hand. "Then he's not gone. Not completely."

"Not if he healed you. But I can't touch him anywhere.

"Shell-shock, I'd say."

"What about that man Stash? The one-handed guy a couple of rooms over. Colin told me he was an assassin." She suppressed a shudder.

"Yes. He's the one I told you was after Colin."

"What did he have to do with you?"

"Well, like most street types with unsavory backgrounds, he had tapped into the underground . . . in this case, Winton."

Amber sucked in her breath. "Winton!

"Yes. And Winton, when he found out I was sold instead of killed, was putting out feelers anywhere he could, including Lasertown. Stash was going to sell me out as soon as he'd done the other job."

"Oh, Jack." She sat very still on the edge of his bed. "He won't quit."

"No," Jack answered quietly. "And neither will I. He owes me Milos and Claron and a lifetime. That Dominion needler the Thraks fired upon didn't get their orders from just anybody. It had to have been en route weeks ago."

"Winton?"

"Or Pepys himself."

Amber stiffened. "Jack! He's sent for you. There's an honor guard waiting at the hotel to take us home."

"And we'll go with them, but with our eyes open this time. I can't act just for myself. K'rok showed me that. Just as he was a commander for the Thraks, he's also one of the last of his race. He didn't hesitate to put the one destiny before the other. I won't either."

"What about Bogie?"

"He'll come with me, too. Before the site was destroyed, I saw—and Bogie through me—this beast, mummified in the rock. It called out to Bogie and he called back to it. It ... shocked him. Amber, I don't know what Bogie is, but I don't think he's a berserker. I think he's something different and something more."

She leaned forward and carefully threw her arms about his neck. "Like the warriors K'rok thinks went after the Thraks."

"Maybe." He enjoyed her embrace despite the sore spots.

"What's ahead of us?"

"First we get Bogie. Where is he?"

"In the shop. The grateful citizens of Lasertown are revamping him absolutely free and—get this—the Flexalinks are getting a norcite plating. You're going to be unstoppable."

Jack smiled, a little lopsidedly. "I'll have to be."

DAW

**THEY WERE THE ULTIMATE ENEMIES,
GENERALS OF STAR EMPIRES FOREVER OPPOSED—
AND WORLDS WOULD FALL
BEFORE THEIR PRIVATE WAR...**

IN CONQUEST BORN
C.S. FRIEDMAN

Braxi and Azea, two super-races fighting an endless campaign over a long forgotten cause. The Braxaná—created to become the ultimate warriors. The Azeans, raised to master the powers of the mind, using telepathy to penetrate where mere weapons cannot. Now the final phase of their war is approaching, when whole worlds will be set ablaze by the force of ancient hatred. Now Zatar and Anzha, the master generals, who have made this battle a personal vendetta, will use every power of body and mind to claim the vengeance of total conquest.

☐ **IN CONQUEST BORN**　　　　　　　　(UE2198—$3.95)

DAW

DAW PRESENTS STAR WARS IN A WHOLE NEW DIMENSION

Timothy Zahn
THE BLACKCOLLAR NOVELS

The war drug—that was what Backlash was, the secret formula, so rumor said, which turned ordinary soldiers into the legendary Blackcollars, the super warriors who, decades after Earth's conquest by the alien Ryqril, remained humanity's one hope to regain its freedom.

☐ THE BLACKCOLLAR (Book 1)　　　　(UE2168—$3.50)
☐ THE BACKLASH MISSION (Book 2)　　(UE2150—$3.50)

Charles Ingrid
☐ SOLAR KILL (Sand Wars #1)

He was a soldier fighting against both mankind's alien foe and the evil at the heart of the human Dominion Empire, trapped in an alien-altered suit of armor which, if worn too long, could transform him into a sand warrior—a no-longer human berserker.

(UE2209—$3.50)

John Steakley
☐ ARMOR

Impervious body armor had been devised for the commando forces who were to be dropped onto the poisonous surface of A-9, the home world of mankind's most implacable enemy. But what of the man inside the armor? This tale of cosmic combat will stand against the best of Gordon Dickson or Poul Anderson.

(UE1979—$3.95)
